NEVER GO HOME

A DCI HARRY MCNEIL NOVEL

JOHN CARSON

MAX DOYLE SERIES

Final Steps

Code Red

The October Project

SCOTT MARSHALL SERIES

Old Habits

NEVER GO HOME

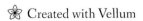 Created with Vellum

For my niece, the real Stacey Mitchell

ONE

Randolph Mays was a huge bloke. 'You're just big-boned,' his mother used to tell him, with a puzzled look on her face. How could her son be so overweight when she fed him all the right things?

'We're going to have to get him to a doctor,' he had heard her tell Father one night, when he was in bed, scoffing a packet of crisps under the bedclothes.

'Leave the boy alone. There's nothing wrong with him. He just likes his food.' Father sat in his armchair, reading the paper, smoking his pipe and drinking his pint of pale ale.

The bad habits had been psychologically instilled in Randolph from an early age, he had once told a counsellor at an over-eating class. He had gone when he was thirty, after his mother had suggested that if any woman was going to be interested in him, she would need to bring her guide dog to live with them when they got married. Randolph had stuck two fingers up behind his mother's back but had agreed to go, thinking they might have doughnuts at the interval. Or the end, he wasn't fussy. So long as they had some.

Plus, maybe it was a place to meet women. He wasn't averse to dating, far from it. But the only women he had met so far had been either his own weight or twice his age.

'Beggars can't be choosers, son,' Father had said. It was alright for him, he had Mother. Sometimes Randolph wondered what the woman had seen in his father; he hadn't stopped to think that maybe he, Randolph, was the end result of a hasty fumble after a barn dance.

He had decided that he would lose weight. The internet was full of tossers bragging about how they had a six-pack and they had started doing yoga to get themselves in shape. Randolph had tried yoga but had only managed to pull a hamstring and had got wired into a box of doughnuts to help him through the pain. Then he had started again, and after a while had started to see some results. His weight slowly went down, and he had started to tone up and didn't get out of breath just pulling some sheets off the toilet roll.

Maybe these guys who were on YouTube with their blonde girlfriends and fancy flats weren't such egotistical bastards after all. Maybe they hadn't just been blowing smoke out of their arse.

It was bittersweet for Randolph after he had lost the weight. He looked half decent now, had actually started grooming his beard, taking it from the badger's arse look to something that might not have appeared on the cover of *GQ* magazine but would certainly have given Desperate Dan a run for his money.

The problem was, all the girls in this village knew who he was, and they could remember the fat bastard slob that he had once been. They couldn't get past the fact that Randolph had once topped twenty-two stone, had yellow teeth and had a beard that any self-respecting colony of rats would have avoided. He was slimmer, well-groomed, his teeth white (they'd never compete with the falsers on a Hollywood celebrity, but they were all fucking fake anyway, and given half the chance, Randolph would have happily knocked them out), but he was still unattractive to the regular girls in this godforsaken place.

Then the Mitchell sisters had moved here. Granted, their brother lived with them too and he was a big bastard, but Randolph wanted to build up the courage to talk to the sisters. He almost managed it a couple of times, then bottled it.

Randolph didn't have any friends. Except one pal on the internet. The young guys his own age didn't talk to him. They too remembered what he had been like. He hadn't been like some Billy Bunter they could have bullied, but a big man who would have ripped their arms from their sockets if he had a mind to. But the Mitchell sisters hadn't been here when Randolph had been plus-sized.

They usually kept themselves to themselves, and only the brother would have a conversation with the locals up at the bar. Randolph wondered what the situation was. Were they all divorced and had decided to pool their money and live together? Or had they never been married and just stuck with each other? He'd known people who had never left home, so it wasn't like they were part of a travelling circus. Nobody had to pay money to see them; they could come into the pub and watch them like he did.

One night, Randolph had the newspaper in front of him while he sipped his pint, and the younger one, Lesley, looked over a couple of times and caught him looking in their direction. He smiled back. It was either that or pull a beamer, making them think he was the village paedo.

He was starting to sweat, no doubt adding to their unvoiced opinion. All he needed now was a dirty raincoat and that would be him all set. He took a deep breath, folded his paper and stood up. It was now or never.

Then the brother broke free from the crowd and walked over to the sisters. He put a hand on the shoulder of the one Randolph was interested in, Stacey. With her red hair and pretty looks. Christ, he'd been so busy dicking about plucking up his courage that he was now about to lose his chance.

Lesley stood up, indicating she was going to powder something in the bathroom, and that just left the big man with Stacey. What was his name again? Randolph couldn't remember. It could have been fucking Bawbag for all he knew. Randolph regretted putting the couple of whisky chasers in his pint earlier. It was starting to make his head fuzzy. Well, the six pints and twelve whiskies were making his head fuzzy.

Then a thought struck him: what if she said yes? Yes, I'd love to have a drink with you, Randolph.

Maybe we could go back to my place, and you could make love to me all night.

What would he say then? Sorry, love, I'm blootered but maybe same time next week? God Almighty, his internet friend had suggested buying some blue pills online, but Randolph had baulked at the idea. What if they were fake? Made of washing powder? He would take one and start foaming at the mouth. That would look fucking good, give the impression he was either overexcited or rabid.

Now he was bolstered by the drink, and he was making his way across to Stacey, eyes focused on her, on the back of her head, her red hair shimmering in the lights of the pub –

'Sorry, pal,' some big bastard said, knocking into him.

Randolph turned round and was about to let the drink do the talking when he realised he was looking into the eyes of the brother. Standing taller than he was.

The man had grabbed hold of his beer, making sure that none of it spilled. While making eye contact, Randolph didn't see the pills being slipped into his pint.

'Oh, eh, nae bother, big man.' Randolph had been spun out of the game like a burning Messerschmitt. He glanced once more over to Stacey, and then back at the smiling man.

'Aye, nae bother,' he said, the wind deciding it no longer wanted to be in Randolph's sails. He gave a weak smile and walked back to his table, as if this had been his intended course all along. He put the pint to his lips and finished it, watching as the two women and their brother left the pub.

Then he heard his stomach making a weird noise, and all of a sudden he needed the bathroom. He got up and rushed through to the men's.

The next morning, it was bright and sunny, just how Stacey liked it. She drank her coffee and looked at Darren over the table.

'I'm telling you, he was making a beeline right for you,' Darren said, drinking his own coffee and tucking into bacon and eggs.

'Lucky you were there, then.'

'I'm always by your side.'

'You put a wee powder in his pint?'

'Pills, aye.'

Stacey drank more coffee. The village was her life now, but she wanted more. She put her mug down and got up from the table and walked over to the kitchen window, looking out over the loch in the distance. At the hills that would normally look beautiful but which now felt like the walls of a prison cell. Then she felt a longing that she hadn't felt in a very long time.

'I want to go home,' she said in a quiet voice without turning round.

Darren stopped eating for a moment. 'Why?' he said, washing his food down with coffee.

'I want to kill the bastard,' Stacey said simply.

'You can never go home.'

His words shot into her like an arrow. 'Never say never,' she said. Then, feeling her anger rise, she took out the piece of paper she always kept in her pocket and looked down at the name written on it.

Harry McNeil.

TWO

Detective Chief Inspector Harry McNeil stood looking at what could only be described as raw sewage sitting in the glass on the kitchen counter.

'It's not going to kill you,' Jessica Maxwell said.

'I'm not so sure.' He looked at his sister-in-law and made a face. 'Please don't tell me you drink this muck.'

'Drink it, clean the toilet with it. You name it, there's a use for it.' She smiled at him.

'Away with yourself. You think I'd rather have that than a bowl of Coco Pops.' He looked over to his daughter, who was sitting in her highchair at the kitchen table. 'What do you think, Grace?'

Grace giggled.

'See? She thinks it's fine,' Jessica said.

'Until you let her try it.' He shook his head. 'Thanks, but no thanks. I'll have toast.'

Jessica laughed and drank some of the liquid. 'Mother of Christ. I think I put too much kale in.'

'What's kale when it's at home?'

'Your ignorance never fails to amaze me,' Jessica said, watching as Harry popped two slices of bread into the toaster. 'Your arteries are going to be complaining forty years from now.'

'If I get tested in my eighties and I have a blocked carotid, I'll tell you that you were right.'

Toast popped, he buttered it as Jessica finished feeding Grace.

'I've got the things for Grace's wee party at the nursery,' Jessica said.

Harry had forgotten about it, truth be told. The get-together with the other toddlers at the nursery he owned and where Jessica was manager. Forgotten, or put in a place in the back of his mind? His daughter's first birthday, and it would be without her mother. Alex had died less than a year ago, and once again on events like this he felt an invisible punch in the guts.

'You okay?' Jessica asked.

'Aye, I'm fine. Just thinking.'

She nodded. 'Alex. I know. I miss her too.'

'Anyway,' he said, shrugging it off. 'I'm sure the wee yin will love it. Thanks to Auntie Jess.'

Jessica hesitated for a moment. 'Morgan spoke to me about throwing a party for Grace. I told her we had one planned at the nursery. She started to insist, but I shot her down. I hope you don't mind. I know you and I had spoken about it and we agreed that it wasn't the best idea, considering.'

'She never mentioned it to me.'

'If she does, she might tell you I was a bitch about it, but I really wasn't. I just had insider knowledge, and I knew what you wanted.'

'I'll confirm to her that you're never a bitch,' Harry told her.

'Now with a bit more conviction.' She tilted her head at him.

Harry stood up straight. 'I swear, m'lord, that Jessica is never a bitch.' He smiled at her. 'There. That better?'

'Not much, but it'll do. But I can't stand here gallywagging all morning. We have work to go to.'

'What's gallywagging? Another word you plucked out of *Jessica's Guide to Alternative English*?'

'Don't use big words, Harry.'

'You're funny. But take care and I'll see you at dinnertime.' He walked over to his daughter. 'Daddy'll see you tonight, sweetheart.' He looked at her smile and saw her mother's eyes in his child.

'Is my tie on straight?' he asked Jessica as he slipped his jacket on.

'Nope.'

'Good. See you later.'

'Not if I see you first.'

Then Harry was gone. He checked his phone to see if Morgan had sent him a text. Dr Morgan Allan, his girlfriend. She had. Christ, he felt like he was sixteen again. The little smiley face emoji meant she had thought about him at breakfast. He sent one back as he got in his car, a new Jaguar F-Pace. It was a lot nicer than the classic Jag he'd had for a long time.

Only two days until Friday, her next text read. *Then the weekend's all ours.*

I'm seeing you tonight still, tho?

Of course. Another smiley, this one with hearts.

Harry's phone rang. It was Charlie Skellett.

'Charlie.'

'Morning, boss. How about going to the fair?'

'I was thinking about coming into work first.'

'*That was my first thought when Elvis called me.*' DS Colin 'Elvis' Presley. '*Then he burst my balloon. This is far from a fun day. Might be a long one too. The fair at the Meadows, boss.*'

'I'm on my way.' Harry hung up and forgot about sending another text to Morgan.

THREE

Summer in Edinburgh was usually a hit or a miss, weather wise. Grab a raincoat or wear a light jacket? Harry had learned his lesson many times and always came prepared for any event, storing all sorts of shit in his boot – raincoat, umbrella, snowshoes – stopping just short of adding an inflatable dinghy.

Luckily, today the sun was out and no clouds were in the sky. He stopped the Jaguar SUV behind a line of police vehicles, including the scenes of crime vans, on Melville Drive, near Middle Meadow Walk.

Detective Inspector Frank Miller walked across to Harry's car and stood on the pavement. Harry could see the carnival on one part of the Meadows, a park that had once been gazed upon by sick patients in the Royal Infirmary, but the hospital was long gone, replaced by luxury flats.

'What have we got here, Frank?' Harry asked.

'It was all fun and games, then somebody got an eye out. Literally speaking.'

'Aye?'

'Jesus, Harry, it's too early for puns.'

'Away. It's never too early for anything.'

They started walking up the pathway that split two parts of the park up the middle.

'You got another "I love you, big man" text again.'

'You make it sound manky.'

'Not at all, boss. I think it's cute. Did you send her a wee smiley back?'

'Shut up. No, I did not.'

'Liar.'

There was a huddle of people on the pathway, all of them to do with the crime. The area had been taped off and people were gathering on the periphery.

They cut through the line of trees and approached the funfair. 'Just like the shows in Burntisland,' Miller said.

From where he stood, Harry could make out the top of the carousel, but the bottom half had been draped in blue tarpaulins. Next to it was a ride for kiddies, little cars that went round in a circle.

'Where are the travellers living?' he asked.

'Round the other side.'

DI Charlie Skellett was hovering about, hobbling with his walking stick, looking like he was bursting for a piss.

'You alright there, Charlie?' Harry asked.

'Aye, boss. I nearly went on my arse a minute ago. My walking stick isn't best suited for rough terrain.' The older DI pulled a face like he'd just stepped in cow shit.

'I said you could stay in the office.'

'I know, boss, but I like to get out and about now and again.'

'Show me where the star of the show is.' Harry walked towards the blue tarpaulins and the head of forensics, Callum Craig.

'You might want to get suited up before going near the victim,' Craig warned. 'It's a messy one. Congealed but still. I know how you rich detectives don't like to get your Armani suits dirty.'

'Away and don't talk shite,' Skellett said. 'If I made enough money for an Armani, do you think I'd be bouncing over this shite-covered dump?'

Craig grinned. 'I stand corrected.'

'Aye, you'd better be. Cheeky bastard. Besides, I'm only a DI. It's the boss you should be looking at.'

'I've hardly won the lottery, Charlie,' Harry answered.

'I don't know, boss. New Jag, fancy duds. I have you in the sweep for being a pools winner.'

Harry looked at Miller. 'What's the pools?'

Miller shrugged. 'Haven't a clue.'

'Pair of bastards,' Skellett said, as the other two men grabbed a paper suit each.

They got dressed in the unflattering attire, and then slipped between two sheets of the tarpaulin and saw the carousel. The ornate animals were shiny and painted in bright colours, fixed for all eternity by a pole running up and down through them. It was a double carousel, two horses side by side. The bulbs that would normally be flashing to attract customers were now dead.

So was the man sitting on one of the carousel horses, his head back.

Harry walked forward and stepped up to the platform where the man was. He looked at the face, at the pallor of the skin, the dark hair swept back and gelled up. An older man trying to impress a young woman maybe. But it was the missing eye that he focused on. There was dried blood in the left socket and blood had run down his cheek and soaked into his shirt.

'Jesus,' he whispered.

'Dale Wynn, in person,' Miller said.

'Looks like life caught up with him after all,' Skellett said. 'You remember his slogan? "Vote for me. It's a Wynn win!" He loved himself.'

'I remember his campaigns to become a city counsellor,' Miller said. 'My dad had a few run-ins with him, years ago.' Miller's father was ex-DCI Jack Miller, now retired.

'Wynn always had a way of slipping sideways,' Harry said. 'I had more than one run-in with him. He thought getting arrested was good advertising.'

'It worked, though,' Skellett said. 'He got himself on the council.'

'Let's see what he was up to recently,' Harry said. 'Was he still married? He was when I arrested him a few years ago.' He threw the question out for anybody to answer.

'I'll do a quick Google search,' Miller said, taking his phone out.

'Morning, sir,' another voice said from behind them. DC Colin Presley.

'Morning, Elvis,' Harry said.

'We've been talking to the owners of the funfair, me and Lillian.'

'What do they have to say for themselves?'

'They heard nothing and saw nothing. Usual stuff. They don't want to be involved.'

'Having a dead man on one of their fibreglass horses means they're involved whether they like it or not.'

Just then, one of the city's pathologists, Kate Murphy, came through the tarpaulin like she was the next guest up on a macabre variety show.

'Morning, Kate,' Harry said. It had been six months or so since DS Andy Watt, her live-in boyfriend, had been murdered, and although they knew she was still hurting, they didn't patronise her by asking her how she was feeling every time they saw her.

'Morning, Harry. Boys.' She nodded to the others. 'How is my gang this morning?' She was already suited up, with her bag in her hand.

'I could do with being on a beach with Grace somewhere, but this is a close second,' Harry said, nodding towards the still corpse of Dale Wynn.

'Do we have an ID on him yet?' she asked.

'It's Dale Wynn,' Skellett answered.

Kate looked at him with raised eyebrows. 'The councillor?'

'The very same,' Miller answered. 'Seems like somebody wasn't very pleased with the frequency of their bin uplift and decided to kill him.'

'I think he had a lot of enemies, didn't he?' she said.

'More friends than enemies, but it was a close call, I think,' Harry said.

'He was married,' Miller said, finding what he was looking for. 'I see a photo of her standing by his side when he was on some platform giving his rhetoric. I recognise her. Pretty but with a big mouth. She didn't take shite from anybody.'

'She was a bloody firecracker,' Harry said. 'She could fight, let me tell you.'

'Maybe she did this to her husband,' Skellett said.

'Was there ID on him?' Harry asked Craig.

'A wallet,' the forensics man confirmed. 'There's a driving licence inside.'

'I'd like a look. I want to see if he still lived in Barnton.'

Craig nodded and left to go to the van where the evidence was being kept.

'You look tired,' Harry said to Kate.

'I'm rushed off my feet since Adam left. They got a replacement, but he hasn't started yet. Soon.'

Adam Dagger was one of the other Edinburgh pathologists who had worked at the city mortuary for years. Now he had left for Birmingham, following his girlfriend, who had been promoted.

'I have to admit, I never thought a woman would tie Adam down,' Harry said.

'I used to be like that,' Skellett said. 'Then I met the wife and settled down.'

'You were an animal?' Elvis said.

'Enough of your bloody lip. I was quite the dandy in my time.'

'Christ, it's not Victorian times, Charlie,' Harry said. 'Dandy? Now that's an image I'll have in my head all day.'

'Mock if you must, but I was a player back in the day. Then one day I woke up in the morning after I'd taken a lassie back to my flat, and she'd nicked my wallet. That was it. I knew I had to settle down. And I did. No more going out with any Tom, Dick or Harry. If you see what I mean. Lassies, I mean. Not Tom, or...you know...'

'Dick,' Elvis said.

'Shut up. You know what I mean. I met Pat and we've been married a long time.'

'Why are you pulling a beamer?' Elvis asked him.

'I'll put a beamer up your arse in a minute.'

'That doesn't even make sense,' Elvis replied.

'You know what will make sense? You getting your fucking jotters.'

Harry laughed as Craig came back with the evidence bag. Harry put a gloved hand in and took out Wynn's wallet and looked to see if there was a driving licence in it. There was and he read the address. He turned round and looked into the distance. 'Five minutes' walk. Two minutes as the crow flies. Marchmont. He must have moved from Barnton.'

'One minute for a seagull,' Elvis quipped. 'They're always faster, especially when you're eating a poke of chips on the beach.'

Skellett looked at him and shook his head, glad the attention was now on the DC rather than his love life. 'Your heid's a seagull,' he added.

'Either way, we'll take a car,' Harry said, watching as Kate was moving around the corpse. He looked at her and they locked eyes.

'Eight hours, give or take,' she said, answering his unasked question. 'Looks like a sharp object was rammed through his left eyeball, and unless he had a heart attack as his killer approached him, I'd be pretty confident that this was the cause of death.'

Harry nodded his thanks. Outside of the tarpaulin, he took off the paper suit and put it in a waste receptacle. 'Come on, Elvis, let's go and knock on a door. Charlie? Go and see if you can issue some threats to the owner, see if they can be more coopera- tive. Take Lillian with you.'

'Threats of violence, or...'

'Or having them closed down. Some fictitious violation. I can make a call to a friend of mine in the council who'll be down with an army of inspectors in a heartbeat.' Harry read the owner's name again, painted on the carousel. 'Tell Brendan O'Reilly that we're not messing about here. He either starts to help or else we'll close him down.'

'Will do.'

'Frank? Maybe go and see how Julie is doing with the rest of the crew.'

'Righto.'

Skellett and Miller walked away from a fake horse with a very real dead human being on it. Harry was glad this wasn't a sight he saw every day.

FOUR

'Nice car, sir,' Elvis said as they approached the Jag. 'F-Pace, isn't it?'

'Yes and no. Yes, it is an F-Pace, and no, you may not eat, drink or pick any part of your body in it. Upper or lower extremities. All bodily gases must be contained within each person; the penalty if any such gases are found to have been released, either intentionally or unintentionally, is a boot in the knackers.'

'Check,' Elvis replied, getting in the passenger seat. 'No picking my nose, my arse or spilling coffee in it. Or farting.'

'Or burping,' Harry added. 'That kind of smell lingers.'

'Experience is a wonderful gift,' Elvis said, clicking on his seatbelt.

'I've never done any of those things in my new car. Grace, however, seems to stick two fingers up to my rules. But she gets a free pass. You, however, do not.'

'These cars are one step away from us all having flying cars,' Elvis said as Harry pulled away from the kerb. He made a right into Argyle Place, then followed it round to Marchmont Crescent.

'Up here on the left,' Elvis said, pointing out the window.

Harry put the hazards on to let a bus go round him, then moved over to the other side of the road to park in a permit zone. He put his police sign on the dash.

'They'll think that card is fake when they see the motor,' Elvis said.

'They'll find out soon enough that it's not,' Harry replied. He looked around. 'Right, where's the stair we're looking for?'

'Over there. Green door. Main door flat.'

They walked over the road and Elvis opened the gate before they went up to the door. 'Posh area,' he said.

'Aye, but he didn't always live here. When I arrested him, he lived in Barnton. Even more posh.'

'This is hardly a step down. I would have loved to have had a flat here. I mean, Claremont Court is fine, but this is Claremont Court wearing a fur coat.'

'You moved in with Amy, though, didn't you?' said Harry. 'She's got a nice flat in the New Town.'

'It *is* nice, and my old man worked hard for his flat, but this place, well...'

'*Right, I get the idea,*' a tinny voice said, '*you like the flat. Now if you're wanting to buy it, it's not for sale. So fuck off.*'

They both looked at the video doorbell, before Harry looked at Elvis. 'Maybe it's the maid,' he whispered. Then he spoke up. 'Police. Can you open up?' They both had their warrant cards out.

A young woman answered, standing blocking their way. She looked like she'd been having a pillow fight all on her own: blonde hair unbrushed, eyes bloodshot as if she'd just finished poking them with a fingernail. She was going for the chic-dowdy look with a baggy sweatshirt and matching jogging bottoms, although Harry doubted this woman ever hit the pavement much, unless it was after getting blootered and trying to walk in high heels and eat a fish supper at the same time.

Whoever she was, this was definitely not Wynn's wife. At least not the one that Harry remembered.

'Has he been lifted again?' she asked. The accent was Muirhouse with a hint of Broughton Street on the way up to Marchmont.

'Has who been lifted?' he said, wanting her to say the name first.

'Dale. Who else? Some BBC children's presenter?'

'Can we come in and talk to you?' Harry said, trying not to focus on the woman's skin. He was sure it looked better in a nightclub with low lights and plenty of make-up slapped on.

She made a huffing noise, like she might be doing thirty years from now if she was a heavy smoker. 'Right. Fine. He said to never let the polis in, but if the bastard had bothered to come home last night, he would have been here to tell you to sod off himself, and since he's not, please come in and feel free to rake around. Except in my knicker drawer. You can search all of his stuff, though.'

'Can I ask your name?'

'Sharon Carpenter.'

'DCI Harry McNeil. DC Colin Presley.'

'Like Elvis Presley?' Sharon asked.

'Who else?' Elvis said.

She uttered another quick 'bastard' under her breath as they stepped into the hallway, and she closed the door behind them. 'Living room's just on the right. Bedroom's right next door to it if you want to go sniffing around. Porno mags are under the bed, but he's just keeping them for a friend, he says.'

'Let's just start with the living room,' Harry said, as Elvis led the charge. *The junior ranks are always first in line to get a stabbing,* he had told the young DC, resisting the urge to shove him in the back to hurry him along.

'I was just making coffee when you rang. You up for one?' she asked.

'Thanks,' Elvis said. 'Just milk.'

'Not for me, thanks,' Harry said.

She walked away and took a right into what was presumably the kitchen or the room where she kept her shotgun.

They sat down, Harry on a chair while Elvis sat at one end of the settee.

'Why didn't you want a coffee?' Elvis asked him.

'Somebody's got to be alert enough to call for back-up after she shoves rat poison in it.'

Elvis looked at him. 'Rat poison?' he said sceptically.

'Didn't anybody ever tell you about the perils of

drinking something that's been opened, like a Coke can, or a coffee? You worked with Charlie Skellett before. I thought he would have had your back. But apparently not. Here you are, going to drink a cup of coffee that's being made out of sight.'

'I just need a wee pep this morning, sir.'

Harry leaned forward and whispered, 'We're here to tell her Dale Wynn is dead, we don't know the relationship and she could have rammed an ice pick into his eyeball. But who am I to judge?'

'Christ. You're right. I'll pretend to have a sip and leave it.'

'It only takes a sip for rat poison to kill you,' Harry warned. 'Or cyanide. It's a female's preferred form of murder. Unless she used a knife on Wynn's eye. Either way, keep your eyes peeled. If she takes a Benny, you restrain her while I escape and call for back-up.'

'Why do I have to restrain her?' Elvis said.

'You're younger and fitter. And because I say so. And if I think for one minute you're going to do a runner, I'll knife you myself.'

'Sake,' Elvis said.

'What are you two whispering about?' Sharon asked as she came into the room with two mugs. She handed one to Elvis.

'Thanks,' he said, looking at the brown liquid for signs of rat poison or any other non-dietary additives, but he couldn't see any and decided to take a chance.

Sharon looked at each of the police officers in turn. 'Are you going to tell me what my boyfriend has done now?'

'I'm sorry to tell you that he's dead,' Harry said.

Her eyes opened wide and she slowly put her mug on a side table. 'Dead? What do you mean, he's dead?'

'He was found murdered this morning.'

Sharon gasped and put a hand over her mouth. 'Murdered. How? When? What happened to him?'

'That's still to be determined. But we have to ask you a few questions.'

Sharon started crying.

'We know this is tough, Sharon, but we need your help,' Elvis said.

She stopped crying and looked at him. Nodded. She wiped her eyes with the back of her sleeve. 'I'll do anything.'

'Don't be offended by this question,' Harry said, 'it's just to rule you out. But where were you last night?'

She looked at him like she was going to argue for a moment, then looked down at the carpet. 'We were down at the fair. We were having a good time, having a laugh. We even went on some of the rides. Then about ten o'clock, it started to get a bit breezy, so I asked Dale if we could come home. He said fine, no problem, it was about to shut anyway. We could grab something from the chippie. But then his bloody phone rang. I told him to ignore it, but he said it was work. He answered it and told me to go ahead and get the fish suppers. He'd be right behind. But he wasn't. He didn't come home last night, and I thought the call was from a woman.'

'He didn't mention who the call was from?'

Sharon shook her head. 'No. Just work.'

'What *is* work these days?' Harry asked.

'He sold off his building company when he became a councillor. He didn't want any conflict of interest. So he invests his money in property and lives off the income he gets from that, plus whatever else he has in the bank.' She looked up at him. 'His future's in politics. Was. He was destined for great things. He was passionate about Edinburgh and wanted to see us be a lot greener. He was furious with how this council was run. So he stood for election and won, and he had his sights on Holyrood.'

'He built houses, didn't he?' Elvis said.

Sharon nodded. 'He did. Good ones too. Green

efficiency, that's what he was all about.' She looked at Harry. 'Do you think somebody from the council killed him?'

'We're looking into every possibility,' Harry answered. 'Do you know of anybody on the council who might have wanted to hurt him?'

'Not really. More likely somebody from his old company would want to take his head off. He worked with some nasty bastards. I was glad when he got out of that game.'

'What about the ex-Mrs Wynn?' Elvis asked.

Sharon curled her lip like she really had gobbed in the coffee. 'Bitch. It wouldn't surprise me if she did something to him. She's a nasty cow. Her and I went at it many a time. She saw her meal ticket walking out the door.'

'I've met her before, when I arrested Mr Wynn, years ago,' Harry said.

'I'll bet she was lippy to you.'

'We don't exchange Christmas cards,' he confirmed.

'If you're looking for anybody who would want to harm him, you should look at her first. And if I find out she did anything to him, you better put her in protective custody.'

'Don't get yourself into any trouble,' Elvis said. 'It wouldn't be worth it.'

'It would be worth it to me.' Her lip trembled again. 'I can't believe he's gone.'

The detectives let her grieve for a few minutes. She excused herself and came back with a toilet roll, pulling pieces off to dab at her face.

'When you were out last night,' Harry said, 'did you see anything unusual? Anybody following you? Did you get into an altercation with anybody?'

Sharon shook her head. 'No, nothing like that. Dale bumped into a couple of people he knew, and he shook their hands. They were pleased to see him. Constituents of his, I think. Maybe people he'd done work for before. I don't know. They were friendly, though. But apart from that, there was nothing else. We were having fun.'

'Is this your place?' Elvis asked. 'This address was on Mr Wynn's driving licence.'

'Yes. This is mine. Dale sold his house in Barnton, and the bitch got half. After she got her pound of flesh, he still had money to live on. But I suggested he move in with me. So he did. It's a lot smaller than he was used to, but you know something? He didn't complain once. He was always a happy man. He loved life. And he loved *me*. We were going to get engaged at Christmas and then make plans to get married. Now I'll have to make plans for his funeral.' A fresh bout of tears, and Harry thought if this woman was a killer, she was a bloody good actor.

'Can I ask what you do for a living?' Harry asked when the tears had dried up.

'I'm a nail technician.'

So is a joiner, Harry thought but kept it to himself. 'When you came home last night, did you see anybody?' he asked instead.

'No. I brought the fish suppers in. I was going to heat them when he came in, but I got annoyed. I tried calling him, but it went to voicemail. Here, check my phone.' She fiddled with the locked screen and went into the recent calls section before passing it over to Harry.

He looked at the call log from the previous night and saw that she had indeed called the same number over and over before finally giving up.

'I'll note that number down,' he said, taking a photo of it with his own phone before handing it back to her.

'Did Mr Wynn stay out before and not come back in?' Elvis asked.

'No. I don't know why I thought he would be with another woman. But I guess why else would he stay out and not call me?'

Harry ran through the gamut of reasons in his head: accident, abduction, murder. 'It happens,' Harry agreed, not wanting to talk about somebody poking something sharp into her boyfriend's eyeball.

He stood up, giving Elvis the cue to do the same. 'Can we call somebody to come round and be with you?' Harry asked.

'I'll call my sister.' Her face was pale, Harry noticed, and she was shaking.

'I need you to go to our station down at Fettes to make a formal statement, Miss Carpenter. If we need to talk to you again, we'll be in touch. Meantime, here's a copy of my business card. Call me on any number, anytime.' *Except on a Sunday morning maybe.*

Sharon nodded and they left the house into a day that felt like it was an oven set at a really low temperature and they were a couple of cupcakes about to be given a roasting. Although Harry wouldn't have been in a hurry to call himself a cupcake. Elvis, maybe, but not himself.

'What do you think about her?' he asked Elvis as they got into the car.

'She's distraught. Her reaction was real. You've seen a lot more people react to a death notice than I have, but I've seen quite a few, and she seems the real deal.'

'I think so too. Now let's go and see how Charlie's getting on with old Brendan.'

'You say that like you know him.'

'I do, Elvis. I've met him before. A long time ago. He's a real firecracker.' Harry started the engine.

'And does DI Skellett know about this firecracker?'

Harry smiled. 'He will now.'

FIVE

'A feckin' dead man on me feckin' carousel,' Brendan O'Reilly spluttered. He was a small man with a big stature, a big beard and a big mouth. 'Which one is he on?'

Charlie Skellett and Lillian O'Shea were standing in a large caravan, or what the Americans called a trailer. It was big enough that it would have to be pulled by a truck and not a Volvo estate. It was glitzy, with a large TV as the centrepiece. O'Reilly's wife, Nora, was sitting on the couch, moving her hands like she was using invisible knitting needles.

'What do you mean, which one is he on?' Skellett said, looking at the small Irishman like he was daft.

'Was it Mary? Or Marie? Oh no, don't tell me this Wynn bloke has plonked his arse on my Fanny.'

'I'm going to give him a boot up the fucking fanny in a minute,' Skellett whispered to Lillian as O'Reilly turned away, pacing to the end of the caravan before turning round. Lillian covered her laugh with a fake cough.

'Which horse is he on?' O'Reilly demanded.

'Could be Shergar for all we know,' Skellett answered.

'You don't understand,' O'Reilly said, bouncing a few steps towards them, making Skellett feel like taking his baton out.

'Then explain it to us.' *Before I ram this walking stick up your rear end for keeping me on my feet for too long.* The small Irishman hadn't invited them to sit, which was fine by Skellett. The place stank like a French whore's bathroom and the smelly wee bastard was starting to get on his wick.

'Some people have a particular horse they want to go on,' O'Reilly said, his eyes blazing now.

'And Willie and Fanny are the top runners?' Lillian said.

'Pardon the pun, DS O'Shea,' Skellett said in a low voice.

'This is not feckin' funny. Once word gets round that my Fanny's been compromised, nobody will look at her. The carousel is big business.'

'Considering I can't climb up on any of your plastic nags, I wouldn't know one Fanny from another,' Skellett said. 'But we have a dead man perched on top of one and I want to know if you or any of the other travellers here saw anything last night. I have two other detectives talking to your staff, but you're stuck with us.'

O'Reilly ran his hand through his hair, the appendage disappearing for a second. Then it reappeared, moving down to the beard, pulling it to a point. 'Me and Nora had made sure the place was closed up as usual. There was nothing amiss, was there, Nora?'

Nora looked at the two police officers. 'Nothing amiss. It was quiet.'

'There were a few stragglers, of course,' O'Reilly continued.

'Do you have security on throughout the night?' Lillian asked, not holding out much hope.

'Only Lachlan. Big feckin' eejit. I knew I should have got some professionals in, but oh no, you said he was fine.' He looked at Nora, who wasn't making eye contact with anybody. 'He's my nephew, you said. He needs a job, you said.'

This was enough for Nora, who got up from the

settee and moved quickly to the back of the caravan and closed a door behind her.

'What makes you say Lachlan's an eejit?' Skellett said.

'Because he feckin' is. Big streak o' feckin' piss. All he has to do is keep his eyes open and keep people in check and call for back-up if there's any trouble, but the trouble is, he's a good-lookin' lad and he's always talkin' to the feckin' girls. Not doin' his job. And now he's got one of my girls in trouble.'

Skellett's brow furrowed. 'One of your girls?'

'Aye. Me horses. I can't stand knowing which one was desecrated.' O'Reilly made eye contact with Skellett. 'They're all hand-painted, you know. They's been in the family for years. Me old man started this funfair, you know.'

'You didn't get a wake-up call from Lachlan the eejit through the night, I take it?' Lillian said.

'I don't know where he was. I mean, he's not going to be walking round in circles for hours, but he's supposed to do his rounds regular, like. We have dogs here, and if they start shouting their heads off, then he's supposed to go and check it out. But we mostly have some feckers taking a piss on the side of one of the rides.'

'The body's been there for hours.'

'We close at ten. We could go on for hours later than that, but we have to shut down then because of the close proximity of the houses.'

'Nobody wants to see your Fanny birlin' round and round all night,' Skellett said.

'I don't see why not. They're all beautiful. Bright lights, music. What more could you ask for?'

'We'll need the name of every one of your workers,' Skellett said, keeping a lid on his thoughts.

'What? Are ye feckin' off yer nut?' O'Reilly spluttered. 'I can't do that. It goes against the code.'

'What code?' Lillian asked.

'The carnie's code, that's what. We're free spirits. We don't answer to anybody.'

'That's fine, Mr O'Reilly. We won't trouble you anymore,' Skellett said.

O'Reilly looked surprised. 'Oh. Right then.'

'But please make yourself available for the army.'

'What army?'

'The army of inspectors who will be descending on this place in the next hour. And revenue inspectors. They'll probably be here first. They get really fucked off with people who try and hide earnings so they don't have to pay so much tax. They'll rip through each and every one of you, and I'll make a recommendation that they check your tax records going back five years. I'll also have the DVLA go through every vehicle you have here, and their road inspectors will check every car, truck and van for possible code violations. They'll suck you in and blow you out in bubbles. And let me assure you, you won't be opening tonight. Or more than likely every other night. And if you don't think I have that clout, then take a look at my face; I'm not some wee plooky bastard who's been in CID for two minutes. I have lots of strings to pull and rest assured I'll be pulling every last one of them. But thanks for your time and you have yourself a nice day, Mr O'Reilly. Oh, and one more thing before I go: a wee phone call to my favourite reporter will be happening, and I'll make sure he gets the scoop on the Carnival of Death.'

Skellett was turning round to leave the caravan, Lillian in tow, when O'Reilly almost squealed, 'Oh, *my* carnies? Of course I can give you the names. I thought you meant that cheap bastard O'Rourke over in Fife. Please, sit down. Don't be so hasty in leaving. I'll have Nora get whatever you want.'

'Now we're playing in the same band, Mr O'Reilly. I thought for a moment there that some men armed to the teeth were going to come crashing through this door, looking for smuggled cigarettes. Bad bastards they are. They'll confiscate your fucking eyesight if they think you even looked at a smuggled pack of fags.' Skellett looked at Lillian. 'Sit down, DS O'Shea. Mr O'Reilly was about to get the kettle on. And if I think there's gob in it, I can assure you, nobody will ever go near your Fanny again.'

'One lump or two?' O'Reilly asked, smiling.

SIX

They were in a huddle, like rugby players about to start charging on some unsuspecting group of onlookers. Skellett was taking a particular interest in one of the horses, looking at it from different angles.

'What's he doing?' Harry asked.

'Looking for Fanny,' Lillian answered.

'I don't think it's a real horse,' Elvis said.

'Shut up. Heid-the-Baw names all his horses, apparently. One of them is called Fanny, and I'm looking to see if it was the one Wynn was on. Ah, fuck it. I can't see anything.' Skellett turned away and joined the group. The forensics crew were still going about their business on the carousel. The corpse had been removed and was on its way to the mortuary.

'Right, what did we get out of the travellers, if anything?' Harry asked.

Miller looked at him. 'Lachlan Connor, the young man they tasked with night shift security, didn't see or hear anything. He said he had fallen asleep, which he often does, but he doesn't tell Brendan O'Reilly or else he'd be sent away.'

'Away where?' Harry asked.

Miller looked at his notepad and then back at the boss. 'Just away. He didn't elaborate. He either meant back to Ireland or somewhere else more permanent.'

'Anybody else hear anything?' Harry asked. He looked at DS Julie Stott.

'Nobody hears anything in these places. They were all sleeping like babies.'

'Figures. Nobody wants to say anything in case it's one of their own, and then that way they can keep the punishment in house. It doesn't help us, though.'

'And there's a million fingerprints on those things,' Skellett said, leaning heavily on his walking stick.

'Get checking CCTV in the area around the time the fair closed. Wynn's girlfriend said they started to walk home about ten, but then Wynn got the phone call. Charlie, you look like you could do with a seat; call the phone company and see if they'll play ball and release the numbers from last night, otherwise get a warrant.'

'They won't play ball,' Skellett replied. 'They never do. But I'll call them anyway.'

Harry gave him Wynn's mobile number.

'Do you think the girlfriend could be involved?' Lillian asked.

'She's a good actor, if she is involved, but we'll keep an open mind on her. But somebody get down to the council and talk to people who knew Wynn. He was getting a reputation for himself.'

'I can do that,' Elvis said.

'Good. Take Julie with you. She can lead.' Harry looked at his watch. 'I have to go and talk to somebody. We'll meet up later at the station.'

They started walking away, Miller walking by Harry's side as they went to their cars. 'How's Jessica dealing with Morgan being around all the time?' he asked Harry.

'It's rough, Frank. Jessica was my rock when I needed her, and now Morgan is slowly creeping her way in. I can't ask Jess to leave. She's the only mother that Grace has known.'

'It's a strange one, right enough. I don't want to

think what will happen if you and Morgan get together permanently.'

'Bridge when we come to it, and all that.' They reached the pavement where their cars were parked. 'How's Kim?' asked Harry.

'She's loving her job, working with her dad.'

'It was interesting seeing her work undercover when she was helping Calvin Stewart with that case they were working on.'

'I think Neil is priming her for taking over the department. Not anytime soon, obviously, but she'll work her way up the ranks pretty quickly.'

'She worked for him in London too, didn't she?'

'Yes. Then as an investigator for her mother in the procurator fiscal's office.'

'How *is* Norma Banks these days?' Harry asked.

'A lot calmer now that she's retired. I still wouldn't mess with her.'

'I don't intend to.' Harry smiled and got into his Jag.

SEVEN

Ewan Gallagher peered through the microscope, his intensity tuning out everything else in the lab. Then he stood up and smiled, snapping his fingers. 'Caroline, call Dr Doolittle and tell him this slide is positive. And tell him he owes me a pint at the golf club.'

'Yes, sir.' Caroline scuttled away to the phone.

'*Sir?*' said Bingo, Ewan's friend and workmate, coming over to his workbench.

'Yes, my good man?'

'Oh, piss off. Fucking *sir*. That poor lassie. She should tell you to take a jump.'

Ewan beamed a smile at his friend. Ever since he had been promoted to assistant head of the lab, it had gone to his head. But he didn't give a toss.

'Why are you wearing your beanie indoors?' said

Ewan. 'And the red sunglasses again. I keep telling you, nobody's going to think you're fucking Bono.'

'Attention span of a beagle's bell-end. I told you the optician said I should wear the red glasses to ease the strain of the overhead lights.'

'It's me you're talking to; they stop people from seeing your bloodshot eyes when you come to work still pished.'

'What? I'm offended. You just broke some discrimination rules regarding disabled people. You'll be lucky if your arse isn't out the door by the end of the day. Unless you buy me a pint at lunchtime,' said Bingo.

'Blackmail, ya wee fucking tadger? Besides, I have enough info stashed on you they'd have a lynch mob waiting for you outside after work. Perv, drunk, wanker – you name it, we have evidence on you.'

'*We?* Who's *we?* You been spreading rumours to the new lassie?' Bingo looked furtively over at Caroline, who was on the phone, either to the doctor regarding the slide or the police with a tip-off.

'Indeed I have not. She's nice, but we're not mates after work.'

'You building up the courage to ask her out?'

Ewan made his best scoffing sound, which only resulted in his spitting on Bingo.

'For God's sake,' Bingo said, taking his red glasses off and wiping them on the sleeve of his lab coat, further smearing them. 'I hope you've not got some kind of pox, monkey or otherwise,' he said, grabbing a cloth from his pocket.

'I never even touched you. You probably sprayed yourself, you talk that much pish.'

Bingo rubbed and cleaned, holding the glasses up to the overhead lights three times before he was satis-fied there was no longer any liquid on the lens. He put them back on.

'Christ, now you look like John Lennon. Or Basil Brush, I can't quite decide.'

Caroline looked over at Ewan. 'That's the doctor informed, sir,' she said.

'Caroline, come here a minute,' Bingo said and waited until the young woman walked over. 'You know you don't have to call him *sir*? He's just Ewan.'

Ewan looked at the smaller man. 'My flabber has never been so gasted. How dare you? Get your things together and be off. You'll receive your last pay cheque in the mail.'

Caroline's mouth fell open. 'Oh no. Please don't fire him over me.'

'He's talking bollocks, Caroline,' Bingo said. 'There's more pish in him than a manky Portaloo at

T in the Park. But you're probably too young to remember that.'

Caroline's face went red. 'Oh. Sorry.'

'No need to apologise, Caroline. Call me whatever you're comfortable with,' Ewan said.

'I'm comfortable with calling him Alice,' Bingo said.

'Shut up. You've already been given your jotters.'

Caroline smiled. 'Has anybody told you that you're the spitting image of Bono with those glasses on?' she said to Bingo.

'Spitting image, yes,' he replied, looking at Ewan. 'Spitting being the operative word.'

Caroline grinned at Bingo before moving away.

'Does she know you've got a girlfriend?' Ewan asked his friend.

'I'm only being a friendly colleague. I wouldn't cheat on my Lexi, you know that.'

'Where's Jane Austen this morning?' Ewan asked, changing the subject.

Jane, aka Nan Anderson, their boss. She was writing a thriller in her spare time and would rush off at times, giving them some spiel about where she was going, but they both knew she was going home to work on her book. They kept quiet and she kept quiet about them having an extra-long lunch break, giving them time to get over to the Robin's Nest pub on Gilmerton Road. Taxi there, taxi back, and they would waltz back into the lab, and if anybody asked where they'd been, Ewan would look like his flabber was once again being gasted at such insolence and give them a wee lecture about how he and Bingo had to consult with doctors and working through lunch was taking one for the team. This had only happened once, and after Ewan had had a word in Nan's ear about the offending miscreant, it had never happened again. As long as they didn't come back blootered or reeking of beer and could string a sentence together without it sounding like they were talking Klingon, they were golden.

'How's the dating going anyway?' Bingo asked. 'You never told me how it went last night.'

'I don't go talking about my dates with women, you know that.'

'So nothing, then.'

'Easy there. Where did that come from? Fucking madman.' Ewan stood with his hands up as if he was being robbed at gunpoint.

'You're the one making an arse of himself, not me.'

Ewan put his hands down and sighed. 'It's not

easy after what happened last Christmas. You know, with...' He nodded his head sideways.

'Yes, I do know. I was wrapped up in it, in a manner of speaking,' Bingo said.

'You're lucky, you've got Lexi.' Ewan looked at Bingo, his eyes widening. 'She's got a sister, hasn't she?'

'Nope. No sister.'

'Yes, she does, lying bastard.'

'I meant, she doesn't have a sister who would want to go out with you.'

'Come on, Bingo. What would the harm be? I mean, it's not as if I'm a hunchback. I earn good money and I can turn on the charm when I want.'

'You just described the best features of a serial killer.'

'Be serious for a minute.'

Bingo peered over the top of his red glasses. 'If I ask Lexi, you owe me big time.'

Ewan grinned. 'I'll pack my banjo away for the night.'

'There you go, fucking starting already with the banjo jokes. She'll think you're not all there. I'll end up telling her you're special and then she'll wonder why I asked her to meet you. This will backfire rapidly, and I'll be the one looking like a right tit.'

'Christ, I'm kidding,' said Ewan. 'I'll tone down the humour. She'll fall in love with me. I'll be funny without telling any of my "a nun walks into a bar" jokes. I can be sophisticated, you know.'

'Sophisticated? When you drink wine through a straw, you mean?'

'Seriously, I will owe you big time if her sister goes out with me. What's her name?'

'Chrissie.'

'Nice. I wonder if I should use an alias. Ewan Gallagher makes me sound like I was in a band in the nineties.'

'What would you call yourself?' Bingo asked sceptically.

Ewan thought about it for a moment. 'Ripley.'

Bingo scoffed. 'Ripley? Sounds too much like Ripper. Were you planning on using the first name Jack? Or just the initials, J.T.? Like, J.T. Ripper. *Jack*, middle name *the*. Imagine being in a bar and you're getting on well with a woman and you ask her back to your place and she says yes. Then the barman shouts out, *Taxi for Mr Ripper*. That would scare them off more than seeing you in your vest and skids.'

'The thing is, what if I go out with her and I don't like her? She'll know my name and then it's all downhill from there.'

'I won't ask her, then,' Bingo said.

'Now, now, don't be so hasty. I didn't say I didn't want you to ask her.'

'If she says yes, then just go with the flow. Besides, Lexi will tell her your real name.'

Ewan snapped his fingers. 'I didn't think of that.'

'If you do go out with her, and you mess her about, Lexi will cut off your bell-end.'

'I wish you wouldn't kid around like that.'

'Who says I'm kidding?' said Bingo. 'It stops me from cheating. Not that I would consider it, but that sort of threat makes me sweat inside. That and the promise of getting a chip pan full of boiling oil poured over my bollocks when I'm sleeping.'

'Is Chrissie prone to violent outbursts like Lexi?'

'Lexi isn't violent. She just doesn't want to be cheated on again. Her ex was a cheater. I reassure her every time she feels like our relationship is disintegrating. Chrissie is getting better now that she's been released from Carstairs.'

'Carstairs?' Ewan said. 'You've got to be joking.'

'You asked, mate.'

'Oh, I forgot to say, I met somebody last night and we got talking –'

'Relax,' Bingo said. 'I was kidding.'

'Right then. As long as she doesn't carry a

carving knife in her handbag, I'll go out with her. Maybe we could do a foursome, sort of like a blind date.'

'You're asking a lot.'

'I could always get a pair of red sunglasses like you,' Ewan suggested. 'Then we could both go out as Bono.'

'They're glasses, ignorant bastard. Why don't you draw on a wee moustache with a marker and go as fucking Hitler?'

Just then, the door to the lab opened and in walked a man whom Ewan Gallagher had thought he would never see again.

'DCI McNeil. To what do we owe this pleasure?' he asked.

EIGHT

Detective Chief Superintendent Davie Ross was walking along the corridor like a man on the hunt. Which he was. He was looking for a woman, which wouldn't have gone down well with his wife if it had been anybody other than DSup Lynn McKenzie. Who was sitting in her office when Ross barged in.

'Knock, knock,' he said, standing at the door, grinning. 'I hope you don't mind me intruding?'

'Please come in, sir. I was about to have a cuppa. You in?'

'No sugar for me, Lynn,' Ross said, closing the door behind himself.

'You lost weight?' Lynn said, getting up and going over to her kettle.

'Actually I have! Thanks for noticing. I'm sure

some of the lower ranks still call me the Fat Controller behind my back, but I've cut out the biscuits with my cuppa. So you don't have to hide your Hobnobs anymore.'

She smiled at him as she turned. 'Hide the biscuits? I don't have any. Like you, I decided I'd like my heart to keep pumping a little bit longer.'

They made small talk while the kettle did its thing, then Lynn poured two drinks. Lynn's 'cuppa' arsenal included a range of teas, some of which sounded like they should be in a sachet lining her knicker drawer. Ross declined and accepted a cup of instant coffee.

'Cheers,' he said, making sure he was far enough away from her desk to give him room to jump out of the way when he gave her the news.

'This isn't just a "pop in for a coffee" kind of chat, is it?' she said.

'No, Lynn, I'm afraid it isn't.' *Shite. That came out all wrong,* he thought. Like he was a doctor who was trying to tell her not to buy herself new slippers for Christmas.

'Is it bad news?' she asked, and Ross was sure her knuckles were getting whiter as she gripped her mug tighter.

'Define bad news,' he said, giving a little chuckle

and taking another sip of coffee. He felt like he was the minister about to ask the congregation if anybody had been dipping into the offering tin but replacing 'dipping into' with the phrase 'borrowing from'.

'Am I being transferred back to uniform?' she asked bluntly.

'What? Uniform? No, no, nothing like that.'

'Thank God for that.'

'But keep the word "transferred" in mind.'

'Transferred out of here? Why, what have I done?'

Ross thought about putting his coffee mug on the desk, but that would give her two weapons to choose from should something break in her brain and the line between boss and subordinate became blurred, so he kept hold of it.

'The brass has been discussing things upstairs. Well, discussing something in particular: Calvin Stewart.'

'Ex-Detective Superintendent Calvin Stewart?' As if there was more than one.

'The very same. You see, he applied to defer his pension and come back to Police Scotland. And when I said the brass upstairs, I meant upstairs metaphorically. It was discussed at Tulliallan. And was given full approval. I heard through the grapevine that somebody higher up than them had thought it was a good idea after he helped with a case a few months ago. Somebody with pull had told Tulliallan to make it happen, and as they all scrambled to make sure their pensions were intact, they welcomed him back with open arms.'

'Here?' Lynn asked incredulously. 'Of course it's here. Where else would it be?' She stared at him as if trying to use some mental death ray, and when that didn't work, she spat out some words instead. 'Is it something I've done? Because I work bloody hard in this place. In fact, and no offence to you, but I help keep this place afloat.'

'None taken,' Ross said, holding up one hand. 'In fact, it's just the opposite; they like you upstairs. But what happened with Stewart, well, that was out of everybody's control. The decision was made so high up, you'd need to look down at Mount Everest with a telescope. But I was asked to go along the road to Tulliallan and give my opinion. I knew I was walking into a trap, and had I said Stewart was a raging nut job, it would have put my credibility on the line.'

'I understand. At the end of the day, everybody has to look out for their own arse.' She sat back in her chair.

'It's not like that, Lynn. Calvin Stewart has been

placed back here. That was a stipulation of his return. They don't want him going to another station and turning it upside down. But we don't want you to be overshadowed by him. Unfortunately, it means you'll have to be transferred out of Helen Street.'

'Where would I be going?'

Ross put a hand up as his phone rang. He looked at the screen and put a finger up, indicating he needed to take this. 'Hello?' He listened, staring out of Lynn's office window, before finally hanging up again.

'That was your guardian angel. It seems like a phone call was made to Tulliallan. I don't know who called, before you ask, but they have power. Plans have changed. You're staying here and Calvin is going through to Edinburgh. Don't ask me why; I don't know any details. So you don't have to pack.'

'Either way was good for me, sir.'

'I know that Lynn.' Ross stood up. 'I'm glad you're going to be here.'

They parted ways and she left the building into a city bathed in sunshine. She'd heard that it was to be a heatwave.

A pub near the station – Paddy McGhee's – was busy with the lunchtime office crowd. She fitted right in and saw him sitting at a corner table with a pint and a small glass of clear liquid. He'd started the pint, not bothering to wait on her, but he'd known she would turn up.

'I've been keeping your seat warm,' Calvin Stewart said, smiling. 'Glass of lemonade too.'

'With a wee hint in it?' she said, sitting down.

'Good grief, woman, I hope for one second you're not inferring I'd buy an officer a drink while she's on duty?'

'I'll take that as a yes. Cheers,' Lynn said, clinking glasses.

'Here's tae us.'

'I don't know who you know who swung that, Calvin, but I'm grateful.'

'I have a powerful friend. When I heard Davie Ross was going to have a word with you today, I called my friend and told him it would be better if I went to Edinburgh and you stay here. Of course, I'll miss my daughter and the wee man, but I'll be through to see them soon.'

'It's short notice for you too.'

'Not really. After we worked our big case, Finbar and I both decided that the private investigation game wasn't for us. So I got talking to my friend. Fin and I had a pint with him and he made a few calls.'

'Where's Finbar going?'

'Edinburgh needs a new pathologist. He's going to be working there.'

'He quit his job,' Lynn said. 'I thought being a pathologist wasn't for him anymore?'

'Being a pathologist in *Glasgow* wasn't for him. Too many bad memories after his niece's murder. Remember, he was originally from Inverness and only came down here to try and find out more about his niece's death. Which he did.'

'You're both going to be working through there. I hope you have fun.' She sipped more of her vodka.

'I wouldn't call it fun, but it's going to be better than chasing cheating husbands.'

'Anyway, thank you for doing that. It means a lot.'

'I'm sure you'll be able to come through to Auld Reekie now and again for a wee visit.'

'Count on it. But I have an idea.'

'What's that?'

'I'm finished for the day. Let's have a wee sesh.'

NINE

'To what do we owe this pleasure?' Ewan Gallagher said to Harry, no welcoming tone in his voice. Harry couldn't blame him; when they'd last met six months ago, Ewan had known a serial killer. He just didn't *know* it.

'This is not official business, but I thought you could spare me ten minutes in the canteen.' Harry could see Ewan thinking about it, maybe racking his brain for possible crimes he'd committed and trying to remember them.

'Okay, I can do that.'

He walked to the lab door and opened it ahead of Harry.

'Nice sunglasses,' Harry said to Bingo.

Bingo didn't answer but just stood and scratched his head through his beanie.

'He looks like Elton John with those glasses,' Harry said, following Ewan along the corridor towards the canteen.

'He'll pleased to know you noticed.'

They walked in and Harry bought them both a coffee and they sat at a table.

Harry noticed there was nobody else close to them, which he preferred, and he thought that Ewan probably wanted it that way in case any colleagues thought he was being questioned by the police again. Maybe they thought he wasn't as innocent as he'd made out.

'What's this about?' Ewan asked, taking a sip of coffee that had a taste that even people in a Third World country would turn their nose up at.

'It's personal. I just wanted to ask your opinion of somebody.'

'Go on.'

'David Allan. Morgan Allan's deceased husband.'

'You want me to speak ill of the dead?'

'Only if you want to.' Harry sipped the hot brown liquid and hoped this wasn't what was left after a mop had been wrung out.

'I read about the Lizzie Armstrong attack. You're going out with his ex-wife and now you're doing the policeman thing and checking up on her before you get down on one knee.' It was a guess rather than a question.

'Not exactly. I'm more interested in David himself.'

Ewan shrugged. 'He was a good golfer. Actually, for a doctor, he was a pretty funny guy.' Ewan looked at him. 'Can I ask you something, Harry? You don't mind if I call you Harry, do you? I feel like we bonded six months ago.'

Harry wondered if Ewan was deliberately being a smartarse but indicated that it was fine for him to continue.

'Do you feel like you're in competition with her dead husband? If so, you don't have to worry. David liked the women, that was his downfall. Yes, he was a doctor, but you're a detective, not a scaffy. Nothing wrong with being a scaffy, mind. One of the boys in the pub is one, and they're hard-working bastards. It's not a job I could do, so God bless him. But I don't think that's the sort of bloke that Morgan's looking for. You're ahead of the game: you have a respectable job, and as long as you're not cheating on her, she'll see you in a better light than her husband.'

'I don't think I'm in competition. I just sense a hesitancy sometimes, as if she's pulling back from something.' Harry sipped his coffee, wondering why he was opening up to this guy who had once been a suspect in a murder case. But he had known David Allan well, and Morgan didn't want to talk about her dead husband. Every time he mentioned him, Morgan changed the subject. She was a psychiatrist, so she was good at head games. But so was he.

'I don't see Cassidy anymore. She still works here, and it's awkward when we bump into each other. Bingo's girlfriend has a sister, so I'm hoping we can go on a blind date. People move on. I'm surprised that Morgan is so hesitant after ten years. I know it was a lot different, though; her husband was seeing Cassidy.'

'It's understandable why she might have trust issues. Was David a player here in the hospital? I mean, did he put it around?'

'No. You have to remember that Morgan worked here too. I think he just had a thing for Cassidy. When we played golf on the hospital team, the guys would all talk about what women they were going out with, and David never bragged because we all knew he was married. Until the day he did. Some nurse at the hospital had got talking to him. They were both married so they were keeping it quiet. Are you a golfer, Harry?'

'I've never seen the attraction.'

'I was going to say, it's just playing around with your friends, but that wouldn't sound good. It's the camaraderie, the challenge, the drinking in the club afterwards. But if it's not your thing, then it's not your thing. The boys are loyal, for the most part. David bragged about Cassidy, knowing it wouldn't go any further, even though we all worked in the hospital. He trusted us.'

'How did she find out about him cheating then?'

'I'm not exactly sure. It wasn't any of us, but maybe one of the other golfers overheard and started a rumour, and that rumour was true. It all ended on Christmas Day, as you know, when he crashed his car and died. After he'd been to the golf club.'

'I thought he had been to see Cassidy that day?' Harry said.

'He had. But the club was open. They were doing Christmas dinner, and there was a party on that night. When he came along to the club for a wee drink with me and Joe and the others, he was half-jaked. Christ, he could hardly walk. We all tried to talk him out of driving, but he knew it was a badge of honour at any golf club, drinking and driving. It was a challenge to see if you could get home without wrapping your car round a lamppost. It was a challenge that David lost that day.'

'I looked at the police report for that day. It was listed as an accident after the car skidded on the ice and hit the bridge parapet.'

'If that's what it says, that's what happened,' Ewan answered.

'But the toxicology report came back with no alcohol in his system. Yet you said he was in the club, drunk.'

'Nobody ever talked about the state he was in that day. Besides, they both worked in the Royal. David was an Accident and Emergency doctor. His friends and colleagues were on that day. Anybody could have tampered with the blood results or had somebody in the lab swap the sample.'

'How could they have swapped the sample?' Harry asked, taking another sip of his coffee.

'Easy. Say I was working in there, you were my friend, and one of our mutual friends called me up and said you had been brought in and they suspected you were three sheets to the wind. I could draw my own blood and put it through. Yes, it would have my blood type, but when the report is looked at, nobody's going to know that isn't your blood type.

The report would be submitted and then it gets filed away. A copy is sent to the procurator fiscal's office and the police file away their copy. Nobody is going to question it when it comes back that the deceased is one hundred per cent sober. It was a weather-related accident. Maybe he was going a little bit fast.'

'He wasn't, according to the report,' Harry said.

'Even better. David Allan was squeaky clean when he had his accident.'

Harry didn't want to talk too much to Ewan about his thoughts. Morgan had said her husband hadn't been drinking before he left the house. He must have had a good few drinks at Cassidy McLean's house. But the golf club was only a few minutes by car from Cassidy's house, so he would have been intoxicated by the time he left there and got to the club. Why would she have let him drive? Maybe he felt alright, and the effects didn't show right away? No, that wasn't right.

There was something here about Cassidy that wasn't adding up. Harry really wanted to talk to her but would put it on the back burner. For now.

He put his mug down on the table. 'Thanks for having a wee chat with me, and I would appreciate it if you could keep it under wraps. Even from your pal, Bingo.'

'Especially Bingo. Wee sweetie wife that he is. But you looked after me when people thought I was a killer. I won't say anything. You have my word.' Ewan held out a hand and they shook.

'I appreciate it.'

They took their mugs to a tall trolley where the trays were put and added theirs to one before leaving the canteen.

'I hope things work out with you and Morgan. She's nice.'

'Thanks.'

They parted ways, Harry walking out into the sunshine. Feeling cold inside.

TEN

Back then

He sat in the office, and it smelled of furniture polish. And death.

'I have your results,' the doctor said. He looked at the other man, who had elected to stand behind the patient.

'Just tell me straight, Doc. I know I don't have time on my side. I've known it for a while now. Don't hold back, just give it to me on the chin. I'm past caring.'

The doctor looked at the patient, studying his face, looking into his eyes, but it was like looking into the rock pool that he'd gazed into when he had taken his little boy to Cramond beach many years ago now. His boy, with the fishing net, in his little shorts and striped tee-shirt. He could remember that day like it was yesterday. Cormack. Named after his Irish grandfather on his mother's side.

His little boy, long gone.

'Look, Daddy!' Cormack shouted. 'A fish!' A little nibbler in his net, but it could have been a five-hundred-pound tuna worth millions for all his enthusiasm.

It was windy that day, but it was warm, and the breeze ruffled Cormack's hair. The little boy smiled the innocent smile of any five-year-old boy as he put his fish into the jar with the water in it. He was full of excitement, full of life. The doctor didn't think he had ever loved anybody so much in his life.

His son was even more precious to him as his wife had had a miscarriage with their second child that summer, and depression had gripped her. She had come down to this beach with her parents when she was a little girl. It held wonderful memories for her.

The doctor thought that bringing her back here

for the day would help her. And it did, to a certain extent. She was sitting on a bench on the promenade away from the doctor, staring out to sea and Fife in the distance.

The doctor looked at his wife, and he thought he hadn't loved her so much as in that moment. He thought everything was going to be alright.

He was wrong.

He turned round to see his son running along the sand, towards the steps that would take him up to where his mummy was. The benches were further along from the entrance to the beach. It was packed with people, even though it was narrower here. The doctor started running, but he was in his bare feet and the sand was unforgiving, making him feel he was running through treacle.

'Cormack!' he shouted. 'Wait for Daddy!'

'I want to show Mummy my fish!' his son shouted back.

Then Cormack was out of sight. *Don't panic,* the doctor told himself. *I'll catch up with him.* He tried shouting on his wife, but she was too far away to hear. He ran and then he slipped, falling onto a rock, feeling a sharp pain in his right leg. He looked down and saw the small scrape, but he shrugged off the pain and started leaping across the rocks, keeping focus on where his son had gone.

He reached the steps now and saw his wife, but he couldn't see Cormack.

'Janice!' he shouted. 'Where's Cormack?' He was waving his arm back and forward so she could see him.

His wife's head snapped round, looking at him. The promenade was heaving, with a couple of food vans and an ice cream cart. The doctor looked round for Cormack and his jar and his little fishing net, hoping to see past the other adults and kids and see the striped tee-shirt dodging through the crowd, heading for Janice.

But he didn't see him. He spun round several times, looking for the little boy. He could see Janice on her feet now, heading towards him, moving fast.

'Where's Cormack?' he shouted again as she was near.

'What? He's with you!'

'He was coming up to see you to show you his fish. He was a few seconds in front of me! Where the hell is he?'

They split up, looking through the crowd, trying to see if he had stopped at a food van or the ice cream man.

Then the doctor saw it: the small fishing net on its pole, sitting on the grass. The jar with the fish in it was close by.

He thought he was having a heart attack as all the saliva left his mouth. He looked round and round, shouting out his son's name, people looking at him now, wondering what was going on. His wife was shouting now too, but her shouts were sounding like screams.

Then they were close to each other. 'You said you would watch him!' she screamed into his face, tears running down her cheeks. Then she fell to her knees as he took his phone out.

A dog walker found Cormack up in the Cammo Estate three days later, just minutes from where he was abducted.

The police asked the public for help, to send in any photos they had taken that day down at Cramond. They pored through the hundreds that had come in, looking for known paedophiles.

They found one.

Tommy McArthur. A woman had been standing on the rocks taking photos of the sea when she heard the shouting. She had taken more photos and one of them had McArthur in it.

The police saw Cormack walking away in the

opposite direction from Cramond. Just walking along, quite the thing. Not looking at or talking to any adults. But Tommy McArthur was close to Cormack. Not looking at him or talking to him but close by, walking in the same direction.

One photo. Tommy McArthur walking along the promenade. Nothing more. Nobody saw anything else. No boy being dragged away by a stranger. No shouting or screaming from the boy.

Just McArthur looking round over his shoulder, giving the photographer a perfect headshot.

McArthur was brought in for questioning but denied everything. The boy walking near him? Coincidence, his lawyer said. There were hundreds of other people walking near the unfortunate child, not just his client. And as the photo showed, he wasn't in any communication with the child, he was merely walking along the promenade minding his own business.

McArthur refused to give a DNA sample and wouldn't consent to forensics looking at his car. With no cause to do so, no warrant was issued. Besides, he had an alibi. He was meeting his friend further along the promenade, a friend who was walking his dog. They were going back to the friend's house to have a few beers.

His alibi checked out.

Everybody and their dog thought McArthur was guilty. He was hounded by the press and by the public.

Then he faded from the public eye.

Until he was found dead in the Cammo Estate, hanging from a tree.

'Your lung cancer is stage four. It's metastasised to your liver and your bones,' the doctor said.

'How long have I got?'

The doctor looked the patient in the eyes. 'It's not an exact science –'

'How long?'

'Six to twelve months is my best guess.'

The patient sat looking at him while the doctor rattled off all the things that would happen now.

'I wish it was better news,' the doctor said, and listened to the man coughing.

'It's life. I'm not going to shed a tear over it, Doc, and neither should you.'

He stood up and they exchanged pleasantries. Then the patient left, and the doctor sat back and thought about his little boy.

ELEVEN

Now

Morgan Allan had just finished with her patient when one of the admin staff came in.

'He's here again.'

Morgan looked at her and nodded. 'I told you before, I don't mind.'

The woman stood up straighter as if she'd been slapped not just slighted. 'I told him before he just can't come waltzing in here whenever he feels like it. He has to go through the proper –'

Morgan held up a hand. 'He called me and I said it would be okay.'

'Well, that's hardly appropriate, if you don't mind me saying.'

Morgan stood up. 'I do. Lizzie might be here because she allegedly killed somebody, but she has rights. It's our duty to see she gets the best care and attention so we can see if she can recover.'

The woman sniffed like somebody had just dropped one in the office and she was keen to show it wasn't her. 'You're the doctor.'

'Yes, I am. And Lizzie is my patient and her boyfriend has stuck by her for more than six months since she was arrested, which is admirable of him. He's trying to help Lizzie. Which we're *all* supposed to be doing. This is a tight ship, Mrs Thompson, and if you feel like jumping, don't let me hold you back.'

'Well then,' the older woman said. 'Let it be on the record that I don't approve.'

'Duly noted.' *Now, bog off.*

The woman got the subliminal message and closed the door behind her. Morgan hoped the door hit her on the arse on her way out.

Morgan put some papers in her desk drawer and looked at her watch before getting up. Lunchtime. But lunch would have to wait. Maybe after Ben had spoken to Lizzie, they could grab a bite to eat.

She walked along to the secure unit, going

through the security area first. She saw Ben Tasker sitting in a waiting room, waiting for somebody to come and get him and take him to the secure ward where Lizzie was. Each of the patients had their own room, for obvious reasons.

He stood up when she came into the room. 'Hi, Dr Allan.'

'Hello again, Ben. Have you been waiting long?'

He nodded. 'They said they would have to prepare her for my visit, that I couldn't just turn up unannounced. So they're stretching it out, just to teach me a lesson.'

'Are they now?' Morgan left the room, walked further along and stepped into the nurse's station, where some orderlies were standing around, chatting. They were laughing and stopped when she entered the room.

'Can I help you?' one of them said.

'I'm Dr Allan. A visitor is here to see Lizzie Armstrong. Can he get in now to see her?'

'I told him this isn't a circus.'

'Did you now? Well, Lizzie Armstrong is one of my patients, and I'd like you to show Mr Tasker in to see her right now.'

The man knew he was on a hiding to nothing

arguing with the doc, so he stood up. 'I'll let you in now.'

Out in the corridor, Morgan indicated for Tasker to follow her and the young man jumped up out of his seat and followed them to the locked security door.

Into the other corridor, they went along to Lizzie's room, where the orderly unlocked the door.

The young woman sat on the bed, her knees pulled up to her chest.

'Hello, Lizzie,' Morgan said with a smile. 'You have a visitor.' She stepped aside to let Tasker enter.

'Hello, Lizzie,' he said.

Lizzie looked at her ex-boyfriend, locking eyes with him. 'I don't want to talk to you. I told you that before.'

'Nobody's forcing you to talk, Lizzie.'

'But I do want to talk,' Lizzie answered. 'I want to talk to Frank Miller.'

TWELVE

DS Lillian O'Shea tracked down Dale Wynn's ex-wife via her work. Which was a nursing home in the Grange. Sarah Wells was the owner and director of the home.

Charlie Skellett opened the passenger side of the car and held on as he got his leg out, looking like he was pished.

'Is your leg not feeling any better?' Lillian asked again. Maybe for the millionth time. Charlie had stopped counting weeks ago.

'It is. The whisky in my cornflakes makes me go all loopy.' He clattered his walking stick about, skelping the door as he tried to stand up.

'You want me to grab an arm?' Lillian asked.

'Oh aye, make me look like I belong in here, why don't you?'

'Suit yourself.' She stood by the passenger door and watched as Skellett struggled to get out.

'Don't just stand there gawking, give an old bloke a hand.'

'I thought you said –'

'Never mind what I said. I talk pish all the time. Don't you know me by now?'

'Well, now that you mention it...'

'That's enough, Sergeant. We'll have a wee bit of respect if you don't mind.'

'You look like you could run away and join the circus with moves like that,' a woman said from the front door.

It had been a magnificent house in its day, before time and real estate developers got hold of it. Stone steps led up to the entrance and Skellett looked up them to the younger woman standing at the top. She was dressed in trousers and a white blouse.

'Trust me, don't think I haven't thought about it.' He straightened up and closed the door and both officers walked towards where the woman was standing.

'DI Skellett, I take it?' the woman said.

'Mrs Wells?'

'Yes. Come in and we can talk business in my office and not on the steps,' she said, opening the large wooden door with the glass panel in it.

'This is a care home?' Skellett said as they walked into the entrance.

'It is. For private clients. We only have twenty-five. We had an annexe built on and there are rooms through there.' She stopped and smiled at Skellett. 'Listen to me; I feel like I'm giving a tour of the place. Please, come through to my office.'

They walked past a reception room where three young women were working away and they followed Sarah through to a door on the left, down a little hallway.

'This is a nice place,' Skellett said as Sarah held the door open for them. They sat in comfy chairs in front of her desk.

'It must have been a beautiful house, back in the day,' she agreed. 'Would you like a cool drink?'

They both shook their heads and Sarah sat opposite them. 'You wanted to talk to me about something but wouldn't say on the phone. Is it about coming to live here?' She nodded to Skellett's walking stick, which he had propped against the side of his chair.

Skellett pegged the woman to be in her late forties, her hair dyed blonde with good teeth that money had paid for. She seemed a nice person apart from being a cheeky cow.

'No, nothing like that. We have some bad news, I'm afraid. Your ex-husband is dead.'

Her reaction took him by surprise: she smiled as she sat back in her chair. 'Oh boy. What did Dale get himself into now?'

'A carousel ride at the carnival,' Lillian said, feeling her hackles rise. 'Somebody took his eye out and left him there to die.'

Still the smile, which Lillian wanted to wipe off her face now. 'Can I ask what you find amusing?' she asked.

'When Dale and I were married, we had chemistry,' Sarah said. 'We connected on a level that only people who are intimate with each other will feel. We were like that; not exactly finishing each other's sentences, but we were close. We had a morbid conversation one night, over a few glasses of wine, and we got to talking about how we thought we were going to die. I said I thought I would die an old woman with my family surrounding me. But we didn't have kids, so any family would be my brother and sister, which is a poor show, if you ask me.'

'And how did Mr Wynn think he was going to die?' Skellett asked.

Sarah looked at them before answering. 'He thought he was going to be murdered.'

They all paused for thought.

'Why would he think that?' Lillian asked.

'Dale was a contractor. He grew bigger and bigger, and when you grow bigger in that line of work, you gain enemies. Dale pissed off so many people, but he didn't care. He had men with him all the time, wherever he went. It didn't stop the threats coming in.'

'We're aware he sold his business to commit his time to politics,' Skellett said.

Sarah nodded. 'He always said he would make a great prime minister. He wanted to start in local politics, and he was a great public speaker. He was passionate about it. But just like when he had his own business, he tended to step on some toes. He sold the business and made a fortune. But if you want my opinion, he was getting a bit loopy.'

'In what way?' Lillian asked.

'Well, not loopy exactly, but he was always beating his chest about his latest pet project: green. He was aghast at what the city is doing, and he said he was going to make it to Holyrood and make a difference in the parliament.'

'What's the city doing?' Skellett asked.

'The big thing with this city,' Sarah said, 'is that they want people out of cars and onto public transport and bikes. Dale thought this was a brilliant idea. And I agree, we have to save the planet. But take a look around you: for the past thirty years, the city has closed streets that were once used as rat-runs. The drivers leaving the city would be able to get out quicker, but now the rat runs are closed off. I don't know how many there are, but it's a lot. Now we have traffic sitting in bigger queues in rush hour, all of them pumping their exhaust fumes into the air in the same spots. It didn't make sense to Dale, herding all the vehicles into roads where they're sitting for longer periods instead of letting them escape the city quicker. And the Environment Agency is a joke. What are they doing about it? Nothing.'

'I never thought of it that way,' Skellett said.

'More and more electric cars are being sold, but what makes the electricity for them to run on? Fossil fuels. And what happens when all the fossil fuel cars are gone? The streets will be clogged up with the electric ones. That's where Dale and I were at loggerheads. He thought electric cars are our future, but I used to wind him up and we'd have heated arguments about the future of transport in this world. I told him that the politicians who want electric vehicles are just after votes so they can line their own pockets. That really set him off.' She smiled, thinking about it.

'Did you see much of Mr Wynn?' Lillian asked.

'Oh, yes. We had lunch at least once a week. That's when we had our little conversations. He really wanted me to be on board with electric cars and I simply can't. My father and I talk about this too, and he's of the old school. He remembers the day when a luxury car wouldn't have anything less than a six-cylinder engine; now they have four cylinders with turbos strapped to them. This infuriates him. Car manufacturers pampering to the politicians. He thinks they're all a bunch of corrupt bastards and he thought Dale would be joining the ranks.'

'Did your father have much to do with Mr Wynn recently?' Skellett asked.

'No. His heart's not up to having a heated argument with Dale. My father knows we have to clean up the planet, but why do the rich wankers still fly around in private jets? His words, not mine. He thinks those overpaid celebs in Hollywood have the attitude "Do as I say, not as I do". I have to say, I agree with him. Billionaires don't have to fly around in their private jets, pumping more emissions into the air than an airliner full of hundreds of people. It's disgusting. I say, fuck 'em. Ban their fucking planes. My words, not his.'

'Do you think that maybe somebody got angry with Mr Wynn because of his outspoken views?' Lillian said. 'We know he got arrested years ago.'

'He got arrested because he had a fight with somebody. Then he got questioned regarding corruption. It was all a farce, really. Somebody up high out to silence him, but it didn't work.'

'Did he recently tell you of anybody who would want to harm him?' Skellett asked Sarah. And then he saw tears spring into her eyes, as if the news had just hit her.

'No. He was very happy. Even with that...thing he's living with. We didn't see eye to eye. She thought I was a bitch and I would quite happily put her lights out. But it's not as if we call each other up every week.'

'Do you think she was jealous of you meeting Mr Wynn for lunch?' Lillian asked.

'I don't see why she would be. I mean, it's a business lunch. Dale owns, or owned, now that he's gone, half of this business. And yes, if one of us died, then the other gets the share. But trust me, this place is not worth going to prison over. It's merely a place I work at and will sell when I retire. I would rather have Dale in my life.'

'When was the last time you saw him or spoke to him?' Skellett asked.

'Last Saturday.'

'You didn't call him last night?'

'No. I don't call him midweek. We have lunch on a Friday to discuss our business together.'

'Can I ask where you live?' Lillian asked.

'Here. I have an apartment upstairs.'

They spent another ten minutes asked general questions, but Skellett didn't think they would get any more out of the woman, so they made their way out, with Sarah promising to call him if she thought of something.

'She looks like she's strong enough to have lifted him onto that mechanical horse,' Lillian said when they were back in the car.

'Aye, she is that, but there's nothing that jumps out about her being a killer. We'll keep our options open, though.'

THIRTEEN

Harry sank back in his couch, feeling drained. Dinner was finished and Grace was playing on her mat to the side of the TV.

'How was work today?' he asked Jessica.

His sister-in-law sat down on the couch with a glass of Coke and put it on the coffee table. 'It was fine. Nothing to write home about. The McIntoshes are behind again. I reminded him this morning how much he still owed, but he said he would catch up.'

'Did he now?' Harry said. 'How far behind are they?'

'Two weeks by Friday.'

Harry shook his head. 'Typical. Is he still driving that Mercedes?'

'He is.'

'I bet when he goes to the petrol station he doesn't ask if he can have petrol and pay for it two weeks later.'

'It's a diesel, but I get your point.'

'Don't be facetious, Miss Maxwell.'

Jessica laughed. 'But you're right; if he doesn't write a cheque by Friday morning, I'll tell him not to bring young Samuel back on Monday morning unless he has a cheque with him.'

'If he has a problem, tell him to call me,' Harry said, flicking through the channels on the TV. 'Anything you want to watch?'

'Let's put Netflix on. We should actually be watching more of it, otherwise you're paying for somebody else to enjoy it.'

'I think they're catching on to people giving out their login details to family and friends.'

'It's not a crime,' Jessica said, smiling.

'Then why do I feel like I've been robbed?'

They were settling down to watch a comedy when Harry's mobile phone rang. 'It's Frank,' he said. 'Sorry. I should take this.'

'Go ahead. I can pause it or fill you in when you come back.'

'Just keep it running. I know what it's about. Boy

meets girl. Boy leaves girl. Girl unhappy. Boy comes back. Boy and girl live happily ever after.'

'When did you become so cynical?'

'It was honed over many years,' he said, leaving the living room. 'Frank,' he said into his phone.

'Harry, I had an unusual request.'

'What you get up to in your own time is your business, son.'

'It's to do with Lizzie.'

Harry put all joking aside now. 'Go on.'

'She hasn't wanted to speak to anybody apart from Morgan. Her boyfriend's been going in regularly too, but from what I gather, she doesn't speak much to him.'

'Ben Tasker. Morgan doesn't talk about Lizzie because she's one of her patients.'

'She isn't one of my patients, so I can talk about her. The thing is, she wants to speak to me.'

Harry was silent for a moment. 'When?'

'Tomorrow morning. I know you can't come along because of what she did in your house, but I thought about taking Julie Stott with me. Just as a witness if nothing else. You know, to listen to what Lizzie has to say.'

'Good idea. I know emotions are still high after Andy's death, so you'll need a buffer there. But are you sure you're up to it? Andy was a member of your team, remember.'

'I am. If she's going to talk to anybody about things and she wants it to be me, I want to do this. Maybe she'll open up as to why she really did it. Or maybe she'll just give me the runaround.'

'On second thoughts, take Charlie with you. It might be better if two senior officers are there.'

'It's a pity that Percy Purcell is away on that course at Tulliallan.'

'He deserves the promotion to chief superintendent, and Calvin Stewart is a worthy successor, I think.'

'I'll take Charlie with me if that's what you want.'

'I do. This could go sideways suddenly if she gets violent or starts her nonsense. Morgan will be there and so will the orderlies, so I think you'll be safe from attack, but I want it done by the book.'

'It's first thing, so we'll be into the office later.'

'Right. See you then.'

Harry hung up and went back into the living room and sat back down to watch the film with Jessica, but once again he couldn't drop his work.

'Is everything okay with Frank?' Jessica asked.

'Lizzie Armstrong will only talk to him. She's been in therapy with Morgan these last six months, but Morgan can't and won't discuss her with me. But now Lizzie says she wants to talk to Frank. Reading between the lines, I don't think Morgan's got very far with Lizzie. That's why she'll only talk to Frank.'

'I'll talk to her alright. Coming in here and trying to Grace. I'll let my boots do the talking.'

Harry put a hand on Jessica's arm and smiled. 'Alex would have been proud of you, wanting to defend your niece like that.'

'Grace is my life. I don't know what I'd do without her. Her and you, of course.'

Harry took his hand away. He loved Jessica, but as a sister, nothing more. Even though she was his sister-in-law, she had become closer than his own sister. He reminded himself he should call her soon. It had been a few weeks since he'd heard from her. And his brother. Maybe they should get together for a meal sometime.

'Anyway, has this guy in the film knocked this lassie up yet?'

'Harry, for God's sake, it's a rom-com, not a porno.' She laughed at him.

'Next time we're watching a James Bond film.'

'Of course we are.'

FOURTEEN

Back then

Ted Williams sat back in his office chair and popped another one of his special pills. For indigestion, he had told his wife when she had seen him taking one in the house. Prescription, he explained, and luckily for him, she didn't get close enough to look at the label. The bottle had held some other medication, but now it was his little bottle of happiness.

He'd been taking them for a while now. And who could blame him? Dealing with the type of clients he had. That's what he had to call them, instead of 'that bunch of fucking mutant bastards'.

His therapist told him that it was better than coming to work one day with a shotgun and letting them have it.

He used to love his work, but he had become jaded when he became the boss. It was what he had aspired to, after all the hard work and, if truth be told, a little cheating and a few incidents of being underhanded.

One example was when the shortlist had been whittled down to Ted and another bloke called Reece. Ted had the experience, the knowhow, the diligence, all the attributes for the job, but Reece was a doctor. A fucking doctor! A PhD of course, not a real doctor, but still, Ted wasn't a doctor. The paper ceiling, they called it. He was going to be leapfrogged for this position, and that simply wasn't good enough.

What Reece had in paper qualifications, he lacked in the real world. So how could he run this ship? He couldn't, and that's why Ted had set him up for a fall, because Ted had found out the man's secret. His appetite for prostitutes. It was easy after that: a friend of Ted's whom he had pulled strings for in the past had agreed to help, and after Reece spent the night with her, the police had been sent to the room to find him unconscious, doped up to the eyeballs. He denied any wrongdoing, said that he'd been set up, but after a quick word with the manager, who had confirmed Reece's preferred pastime, Reece was arrested and his run to be the boss had come to an abrupt halt. And Ted had walked into the job.

Now he was captain of this ship, but it didn't come without its headaches.

Like the Gorilla – his assistant – waiting on the other side of the door with one of the mutants in tow. Luke Silver was a big bastard. Ex-army, arms like tree stumps and a face that looked like it was still being skelped, he stood at over six-five. Nobody ever gave him hassle, not unless they wanted their private bits inserted into their body by the tip of a boot.

The particular man Ted was seeing today was sick. Ted didn't really give a toss, at least not until his little pill kicked in. Then he would pretend to be nicey-nicey.

Ted pressed the intercom button and told the secretary to usher Silver and his charge into the office.

Silver always entered a room like he was expecting a hand grenade to go off, looking furtively around as if Ted was harbouring some chainsaw-wielding maniac who was about to cut them all into little pieces.

'Morning, Te...sir,' Silver said. Ted locked eyes

with the man. They'd talked about this first-name thing before, but obviously he had the attention span of an ant's arsehole.

Silver, unfortunately, knew of Ted's little pill habit. One day he had plonked himself down in the chair opposite Ted. Ted had spluttered and showed indignation until Silver fired out the name of the pills Ted was on, and after that they did the dance where Ted denied everything and Silver told Ted what he wanted in return for his silence. Ted gave in, not happy he was being blackmailed by a man who had the intelligence of a house brick. It was worth it to have Silver on his side, and things had been running smoothly ever since.

The man came in, wheeling an oxygen tank behind himself. He looked like absolute shite, and Ted made a mental note to have his whole office cleaned after this visit, if not burned to the ground.

'Sit, sit,' Ted said, almost blurting out 'manky bastard' but keeping it in check. He met Silver's eyes and he could tell the big man agreed. Ted would hear what this filth-bag had to say, then let him be on his way.

The man sat and coughed, and when he finally raised his face, his eyes were red, which made him look like some sort of werewolf. Not a scary one, but one that had been out on the piss the night before and smoked a packet of fags for breakfast.

'Would you like a drink?' Ted asked, more for his own well-being than the man's. If he wasn't coughing, then he wasn't spreading germs about like he had the Spanish flu.

'Thanks,' the man said, and Silver picked up the bottle of water from where Ted had told him it would be before he had left to bring the man in. It was beside a plant, which would have seen the contents of the bottle if Typhoid Mary hadn't wanted it.

Silver handed the bottle over, and the man drank from it.

'I see you're going home today. I just wanted you to know that I wish you the best of luck.'

'I'm fucking dying, not moving on to another job.' He swigged at the water, and started coughing again, and Ted thought the man was going to vomit all over the office, but he merely released some contagious pathogen into the air instead.

'Yes, well, I wanted to give you this before you went.' Ted picked up an envelope that had been sitting on his desk and held it out for the man to take, but he had to wait until the next attempt at boaking up a lung had subsided.

'What's this? You had a whip round?' The man snatched the envelope, his voice sounding like he'd gargled with sand.

'You could say that. It's from Her Majesty. She heard about you and felt sorry. She sends her best.'

The man curled a lip and thought about opening the envelope, but the coughing fit that appeared to have worked its way up from his boots reached his mouth and he merely put the envelope away in his pocket.

'I would like to say it's been a pleasure,' he said, 'but you know how that goes.' He stood up on feeble legs and looked at Ted. 'I won't shake your hand. Wouldn't want you to catch anything.' He turned to go, wheeling his tank behind him.

Damn fucking straight you won't, Ted thought, but merely smiled. 'You want my advice?'

The man stopped and turned slightly. 'What's that, then?'

'Enjoy the rest of your time. Don't die a bitter, twisted man.'

He looked at Ted and smiled the smile of a dead man. 'Oh, I will. You won't believe how I'm going to enjoy myself.'

And with that, he was gone. Ted thought he would never see the man again.

He was wrong.

FIFTEEN

Now

It was a song on the radio that sparked this feeling off. D:Ream, 'U R the Best Thing'. Stacey Mitchell had looked around her, at the people in her life, at the village they lived in, their house. None of it screamed out at her to stay here.

'You okay?' her brother, Darren, said.

'I just feel a bit off today, that's all.'

'You want me to get you something?' Lesley asked.

Stacey patted her stomach as she pushed her chair away from the kitchen table. 'I think I just have an upset stomach. I'll make a cup of tea and see if that helps.'

'Pop a couple of tablets,' Darren said. Which he would say, of course, since he was in charge of anything pharmaceutical apparently. Randolph would have woken up with a bad taste in his mouth but no memory of what had happened the night before, except that he'd had too much to drink.

'I will. I think I'll go and have a lie-down, even though I haven't been up long.'

'Fine, well, you know where we are if you want us,' Darren said, flipping through the newspaper on the table.

Stacey put a hand on his shoulder. 'I know.' He would be in his home office, playing around on his laptop. Lesley worked from home too, in a little home office on the ground floor.

Stacey went up to her room, where she sat on the bed, reading a book. But she wasn't reading it; her mind was elsewhere, not on the troubled woman within the pages.

She sat and listened for a little while, looking at her watch. She would have to make her move soon if she was going to make it in time.

Her bag was already packed, ready to grab, just

like a prepper. There might not be any zombies coming, but she was prepared if any should show up on her journey.

She put on her light rain jacket and stood by her bed, her hand on the handle of the bag. Her nerves were alive. She couldn't believe she was doing this, but her anger was driving her forward. No, not anger; it was more than that. Complete and utter rage. That was what was driving her.

She quickly lifted the bag off the bed and opened her room door quietly and made her way downstairs. Darren and Lesley were nowhere to be seen. She made it to the front door, where she turned the handle and the door opened. They had security cameras, like a lot of people these days, and you could sit and stare at the images on your iPad if you had a mind to, but she doubted the other two were watching. Why would they?

She gently closed the door behind her and walked out. This would be the test; there would be shouts and screams maybe if they saw her leaving. But she walked down the path and out the gate. Then down the track to the small, narrow road that ran past their house to the loch. In the opposite direction the street led down to the main road, where she could put her hand out for the bus.

She hurried now, keeping her head down, not daring to look back. The sky was clear, but there was a wind coming off the loch, finding its way over the hill, ruffling her red hair.

Then she was at the main road and she looked at her watch, willing the single-decker bus to come round the bend in the road further along.

'Come on, come on,' she said, almost jumping up and down.

Then it appeared. And the driver smiled as she asked for a ticket to the train station.

She sat down on the opposite side of the bus, not daring to look out at the house. It would have broken her heart to have seen Darren and Lesley run out and jump into the Land Rover and come tearing down the hill after the bus, pulling it over and jumping out –

The bus moved away and she looked across the aisle, sneaking a peek at the house, but of course it was higher up and she couldn't see it. They were off, and there was no high-speed chase, no accusations, no lecture. Nothing.

She settled back in her seat and dozed off, dreaming of a man in Edinburgh. And then the anger kicked in again, waking her up. She looked out at the passing countryside. The man was in her thoughts all the time, never far away. She could feel the rage burning inside of her. She thought of him again as the bus got closer to the train station.

Harry McNeil.

Dead man walking.

SIXTEEN

Detective Superintendent Lynn McKenzie felt happier than she had in a long time. For once, waking up hadn't meant the only company she had was the sound of her favourite morning DJ trying to entertain her – and thousands of others – with classic tunes, between traffic and weather.

This morning she was humming along to a song from the '80s as she poured milk into the two coffees. She had showered and dressed first, and she had heard the shower going off a few minutes ago and knew he wouldn't take as long to dry off as he didn't have long hair to dry like she had.

He came into the kitchen just as the toast popped. 'I wasn't sure what you ate in the morning, so I put in a couple of slices for you,' she said, turning round to look at him.

'Greatly appreciated,' Calvin Stewart said, smiling at her.

She didn't know why his being here excited her, but it did. A man whom she had previously disliked had spent the night and she had laughed and cried with him and seen a completely different side to him.

'You didn't just spend the night because you stepped in and made them keep me here in Glasgow while you have to go and live and work in Edin-burgh, did you?' The thought had jumped into her head like an express train and she felt a little bit of panic grip her.

He raised his eyebrows 'Of course not. I have morals.'

'The last time you said you had morals, you said you had them in the morning with milk. Instead of Rice Krispies. Oh God, maybe this was a –'

He put a finger on her lips before taking it away and giving her a kiss. 'I spent the night because you asked me to. And because I wanted to. Not because it was some sordid wee fling. I've liked you for a long time, but always kept it professional. We had a wee drink, and I think you'll agree, we had a good time.'

She smiled and put her arms around his neck. 'I

did. Before, I thought you were one of those old-school detectives who swore and drank too much, but I got to see another side of you, the fun side of you, and I really liked it.'

'People think I'm an opinionated loudmouth with no manners. But that's just my mother. Everybody else thinks I'm a hoot. Except my ex-wife. She has a special set of names for me.'

'I could think of a few names for you, but I wouldn't repeat them in the station.' She kissed him again before pulling away. 'We'll see each other again, won't we?'

'Of course we will. We've been having a drink socially for the past few months, but last night we went one step further. It would have been a whole different can of beans if I'd still been at Helen Street, but now I'll be in Edinburgh, and it's only forty minutes away.'

'Have they found you accommodation yet?'

'They have. You might not know this, but Harry McNeil has a flat in an area across from the station. Comely Bank. He rents it out and it's been empty for ages. He's particular about who he rents it out to and an agency takes care of it for him, but he gave them my name. I suggested it to him, and the cronies upstairs made it happen. It's fully furnished, so I'm renting my own flat out and my daughter's getting it cleaned for the first tenant. Luckily, the wee man's on school holiday and he's happy to be helping clean Grandad's flat.' He laughed. 'That makes me sound like an old codger, doesn't it?'

'Not that old. I'm turning fifty in a couple of months.'

'Is this the part where we say, age is only a number? Because sometimes I feel my age, and you know how old I am.'

'I'm no spring chicken, Calvin. I like you just the way you are. I can't wait to meet your daughter and her son.'

'Eddie will like you. So will Carrie.'

She stepped back and looked at him. 'Listen to me wittering on. You spent the night and already we're planning Christmas dinner. I'm sorry. It's been a long time since I was in the company of a man.'

'You don't have to be sorry. I didn't spend the night just to wave goodbye the next morning. We can have a proper meal out and a few drinks. If you're comfortable with that.'

'Of course I am. I really saw a different side to you, Calvin. A side I didn't know existed. One that I like.'

He laughed. 'Sometimes the gruff exterior has to

come into play at work or else those baw-heids upstairs will jump all over me. I'll keep you right. Davie Ross is a good guy, tough but fair. We all have skeletons in the closet and I know a lot of his by their first names, so he won't give you any guff. No special treatment either, but he's not one to start making crap up and use it to empty you out the door, like his predecessor tried with me. But I do have a side that few people get to see.'

She smiled. 'I feel lucky that I'm the one who gets to peek behind the curtain.'

'I have to admit, I really enjoyed your company last night, and I mean before we came here. Now, where's the kettle. I'll make you...what? Tea or coffee?'

'Coffee. They're made. Butter's in the fridge.'

'Next time I'll make the coffee. And there's nothing stopping you coming through to Edinburgh at the weekend sometimes. It's not as if Harry lives across the landing.'

'Yeah, let's do that. It'll be fun.'

Stewart looked at his watch. 'Right then, let's get breakfast. I had a call from Davie Ross telling me that there's a shout at an industrial estate.'

'Oh, crap. We should get going.' Lynn looked worried for a second.

'Sit down and enjoy your coffee. That's one of the key things: don't just start dancing when they pull the strings. You'll be the one running the show from the ground, doing all the hard work so they can look good. Fuck 'em. Make them wait.' He looked at her. 'Oops. Sorry. I'll make an effort, I promise.'

'If you didn't swear, I would think there's something wrong.'

'I'll keep it for work, not when I'm in the company of a lady in our own time.'

'You're not on recreational drugs, are you?' She smiled.

'What I'm feeling now you can't buy.'

'God, Calvin, are you never going to stop surprising me?'

'Oh, I've got a lot of surprises up my sleeve.' He grabbed the tub of spreadable butter from the fridge and they sat down at the little table in the kitchen. 'One of them is not rushing to a shout. The guy's deid. Us breaking our necks getting there isn't going to revive him. He's not going anywhere.'

'I used to jump when they shouted when you'd left the force,' she admitted.

'They wanted you to play by their rules. Now you're playing by your own rules, except they don't know it. They *think* you're playing by theirs, but *you're* in control.' He spread the butter and cut the toast.

'You're not as daft as you look,' she said, laughing.

'I am,' he replied. 'I am.'

SEVENTEEN

'I've discovered I have a new talent,' DS Robbie Evans said.

DCI Jimmy Dunbar looked at his younger colleague from the passenger seat. 'What now?'

'I'm a psychic.'

'Psycho, more like.'

'Naw, I mean I'm a psychic. I can look into a glass ball and tell the future.'

'Tell me what the numbers are for the next lottery jackpot.'

'I'm good, but I'm not that good,' Evans said.

'You're just shite, then.' Dunbar shook his head. 'Do you read books on how to be this daft? Fucking psychic.'

'Seriously. It's a gift. Let me hold your hand.'

'Fuck off.'

'I'm serious. Just for a few seconds,' Evans said.

'And what would happen if a patrol car pulled up and they saw us in this car holding hands? I'd put my boot so far up your arse, you'd be tying my laces with your tonsils.'

'That's okay. I can just look into your eyes and it will be the same.'

'Look, ya fuckin' bawbag, is Vern not doing it for you anymore? I need to have a word with her.'

Evans stopped at a traffic light. 'Jesus. I just had a vision of some people carrying a coffin.' He looked at Dunbar. 'It was nice working with you.'

'Shut your pie hole. You're being a creepy bastard now.'

Evans laughed. 'Should have seen your face, boss. But seriously, Vern is into all that stuff. She said she can detect something in me.'

'What, that you're a gullible bastard?'

'No, she says she can detect I have the gift just by looking at me.'

'You won't want to look in the fucking mirror when I'm done with you. Wee bastard. Stop talking shite and just drive.'

Evans laughed and pulled away. Ten minutes later, they pulled in at the side of a street in the industrial estate. The side road was blocked off with police tape, a uniform standing guard. He recognised the two detectives and lifted the tape.

The unit was small, sitting next to a much larger one that had been shuttered for a long time by the looks of the overgrown car park. There was a forensics tent in the small car park at the front of the business, next to overgrown bushes from the bordering property. A woman and man stood slightly back, the man in a suit.

'That looks like...' Robbie Evans started to say. 'It can't be. He's retired. Phew. For a minute there, I thought it was –'

DSup Calvin Stewart turned round just as they approached. 'About fuckin' time. Why are you late? Were you holding hands in the fuckin' car or something?'

'Maybe he's a psychic,' Dunbar said.

DSup Lynn McKenzie turned round as well, ignoring Stewart.

'Holding hands?' Evans said. 'I didn't think you would be talking that kind of pish now you're enjoying your twilight years, Calvin.'

'I forgot to mention that Calvin is back on duty,' Dunbar whispered.

'What? Oh, Christ,' Evans said in a low voice. 'You could have told me.'

'I thought you would have seen it in your crystal ball.'

'That's funny.'

Stewart looked at Evans. 'I see the standard has dropped since I was away. Lack of fucking respect for a senior officer. Well, it better pick up soon. And call me Calvin again and I'll boot you in the fucking bollocks.'

'Sorry about that, sir. A wee bit of miscommunication. It won't happen again.'

'Aye, well, miscommunicate again and you'll be talking like a fucking wee lassie, and no' just at the weekend.'

'It was a fancy dress party,' Evans explained, 'and I was dressed as Woody from *Toy Story*. Vern was Little Bo Peep.'

'Not cosplay, then?' Dunbar asked as they got closer to Stewart. 'I do know what that means, despite me being an old bastard.'

'What are you two whispering about?' Stewart said. 'I hope it's none of your filth, Evans. I mean, what you get up to in your own time is your business, but if it involves you wearing high heels again, keep it for after work.'

'Again?' Evans said.

'Right, shut your hole and listen up. DSup McKenzie here is in charge. I'm here because I was called here. I'm transferring to Edinburgh tomorrow to head up the Fettes crowd – I'll be Harry McNeil's boss – but today I'm based out of Helen Street. Those bawbags upstairs thought this would be some old jakie deid after choking on his own vomit, but that's not the case. Hence the call went out to you, Jimmy, and Dame Edna Everage there.'

'Who's that?' Evans asked.

'That's what Google's for, son,' Dunbar said. Then, to Lynn: 'What do we have here, ma'am?'

'This is an old electrical component building, shut down six months ago. It's being emptied out since it was sold. A sound-editing company is coming in. They have skips and industrial bins here to dump the stuff, and one of the workers found a body lying in a skip this morning.'

'Was there ID on him?'

'Yes. His name is Hamish McKinley.' Lynn stood looking at Dunbar for a moment, like it was quiz night and this was a question he should have known the answer to.

'He was one of the raincoat brigade,' Stewart added. 'His friend Tommy McArthur was accused of abducting and murdering a wee boy years ago. They had nothing on him, no forensics, no witnesses. Somebody had taken a photo of him down on Silverknowes promenade in Edinburgh and Heid-the-Baw there gave him a cast-iron alibi. Then the paedo was found dead in the woods in Edinburgh. Hanged himself. Case closed.'

'We ran this McKinley's name; he was originally arrested for indecent exposure,' Lynn explained. 'The witness didn't turn up in court, so he walked free.'

'And now somebody's killed him,' Stewart added, unnecessarily.

'McKinley lived in Edinburgh,' Lynne said.

'What was he doing through here in Glasgow?' Evans asked.

'We'll hopefully find out,' Lynn answered. 'And why the killer killed him here.'

'He wasn't just dumped?' Dunbar said.

'No. He was lured here and murdered,' Dr Fiona Christie said, coming out of the tent. She was one of Glasgow's pathologists. 'There's plenty of blood around, so he definitely donated it here. I'd expect bruises if he was being abducted and he fought back, but there are none. He was stabbed in the throat and bled out very quickly. There's arterial spray both in and outside the bin. Very nasty. Looks like he knew his killer, and they got up close and took him by surprise. Somebody strong enough o lift him into there.'

Stewart looked around at the ratty old buildings. 'Somebody had something important to say to make him turn up here.'

'I don't see any CCTV on these buildings,' Dunbar said. 'Maybe back in the day, but a lot of them look like they're about to fall down.'

'The area's being regenerated,' Lynn said, 'and not before time, but a lot of the buildings have been lying empty for a long time. So everything would have been disconnected.'

'How long do you think he's been dead?' Stewart asked.

'Three, maybe four days,' the pathologist said. 'It's hard to tell with the heat, but he's rank.'

'We'll have to go through to Edinburgh,' Stewart said. 'Obviously, I was going there anyway, but I want some of your men there, Lynn, if you're okay with that?'

'Absolutely. DI Dunbar, you can take DS Evans, since you're the liaison team with Edinburgh now.'

'Okay,' Dunbar said. 'We can help the Edinburgh team look into McKinley and see if any family member of his victim was angry enough at him to end his life.'

'Give DI Lisa McDonald a shout to get over here,' Stewart said. 'Does she know I'm back or should I brace myself for another round of verbal abuse from a member of the lower ranks?'

'I'll give her a heads-up to spare you, sir,' Dunbar said.

'Much appreciated, Jimmy.' Stewart turned to Lynn. 'Do you want to give Harry McNeil a call since this is your case through here?'

'Maybe you should do it since he's one of your team.'

'Fair enough. I'll prepare him, although we've already spoken on the phone, of course. I can't just step into the station and start shouting orders. He's pleased that I'm coming through to work with them. Shut it, Evans.'

'I didn't say a word.'

'I knew what you were going to say before you even thought about it.'

'He's much better at this crystal ball lark than you are,' Dunbar said.

Stewart looked at Fiona. 'Dr Christie, I'll be out of your hair once again. I'm moving to Edinburgh, in case you hadn't heard.'

'I actually didn't hear. Best of luck to you, Calvin.'

'Thank you.'

'You up for a wee sesh tonight?' she asked.

Stewart looked at Lynn quickly before smiling at the doctor. 'Thank you, but I'll take a rain check. I'm spending time with my daughter and grandson.' It wasn't exactly a lie; he was planning on calling Carrie later.

'Maybe when you come through, then.'

'Count on it.' Stewart gave Lynn a fleeting glance, confirming their date for that evening.

'Are you coming through to Edinburgh with us, sir?' Evans asked.

'I said I'm transferring tomorrow. Besides, I'll drive myself through. No disrespect, son, but if I want to see my life flashing before my eyes, I can hoor up behind a bus doing a ton, turning my underpants broon all on my own, without you having to do it for me.'

'In my own defence, sir, that was a school bus, and the wee bastards were sticking the vickies up at me,' Evans said.

'I don't give a toss if the fucking Yorkshire Ripper was on that bus waving a hammer about. You're supposed to be on a level above that behaviour, no' make it look like we were trying to hijack the fucking bus.' Stewart shook his head. 'A lesser man would have had to go and lie down in a dark room. Jimmy there had to deploy the sick bags.'

'Sick bags?'

'Aye, Tesco carrier bags. I nearly threw my lunch at those kids, and I'd already eaten it half an hour before. Poor Jimmy there had to walk with a Zimmer for a week after he jammed his right foot onto the invisible brake pedal in the passenger side.'

'Zimmer? Don't talk –'

'Were you no' listening when I was talking about respect a minute ago? Attention span of a badger's arse.' Stewart tutted and turned back to Lynn. 'I'll call Harry again and then I'll go straight through first thing in the morning.'

'Okay.'

Dunbar walked away to start issuing orders and Evans caught up with him. 'You might have given me a heads-up.'

'I literally just found out this morning, son.'

'At least he's going to Edinburgh.'

'Evans!' Stewart shouted.

Evans turned round to look at him. 'Yes, sir?'

'I'm no' fucking deef!'

EIGHTEEN

DI Frank Miller looked out of his living room window down onto the High Street and pictured his deceased wife's funeral cortege stopping outside what had been their station years ago. She had been dead a long time and now their station was closed. Time moved on, things changed, and Miller didn't know why he was thinking about Carol again. Of course, he still laid a wreath at her gravestone at Christmas and other special occasions, but if his wife now, Kim, found out, she wouldn't be pleased.

'What are you thinking about?' she asked, coming across to him and putting her arm around him.

'Andy Watt,' he lied, turning round to face her. 'I have to go and speak with Lizzie Armstrong this morning. Morgan has been her therapist, and she and Lizzie's boyfriend, Ben Tasker, have been trying to talk to her. But she hasn't responded to anybody, but now she wants to talk to me. Harry agreed that I should go alone and see what she has to say.'

Kim pulled away, her smile dropping. 'Maybe you could ask her why she chose to come back for a second time and finish Andy Watt off.' She gritted her teeth. 'That was a senseless killing. Andy didn't deserve that. Let me go and talk with her. All I'd need is five minutes.'

Miller smiled. 'I know she wouldn't even last five minutes, but I want to hear what she has to say.'

'What about her mother? Hasn't that murdering bitch got anything to say?'

'Technically, stepmother.'

'Don't be all pedantic on me, Miller. The woman got her own stepdaughter involved in her nefarious plot, playing on the fact that Lizzie had mental health problems.' She gently poked him in the chest. 'Problems that were well concealed, even from poor Paddy. God rest his soul.'

'It's been hard for everybody, Kim. Losing Paddy Gibb, then Andy Watt.'

'I know. Meantime, Maggie Parks gets to

languish in prison while her stepdaughter is locked away in a psychiatric unit. It hardly seems fair.'

'I don't want to get into all this again, Kim. We do our job and then it's up to the courts to do theirs. Yes, it's an antiquated system, but it's one we have to live with just now.'

'I know.' Kim let out a breath, like air escaping from a balloon. 'I still feel angry about how Paddy and Andy died. That's never going to go away.'

Then Emma, Miller's stepdaughter, ran into the room. 'Hurry up, Mum. Annie and I want to go along to Grandpa Jack's now!'

'We're going, sweetheart,' Kim said. 'I have to get your sister ready. Five minutes.'

'I'm away to work,' Miller said, pulling his jacket on. He kissed Emma on the forehead. 'Be good for Grandpa Jack and Grandma Sam.'

'We will.'

Miller kissed Kim goodbye and went down to Cockburn Street, where his car was parked. The drive up the hospital in Morningside didn't take as long since he was going against the rush-hour traffic.

Parking at the rear of the hospital outside the secure unit, he was gripped by a sudden feeling of sadness. How had it come to this? He had met Lizzie on many occasions when he had been at Paddy's place to have a drink. Maggie had been head of forensics in Edinburgh. One of them. How could this have all turned to shite in such a short time?

But it wasn't a short time, he thought, walking across the car park. What Maggie had done had been brewing for years. Though there had been no signs of Lizzie's mental health issues that Miller had observed.

He made his way in and up to the top level, where Morgan Allan would be waiting for him. When he got there, it was a circus. People were rushing about, some on phones, others shouting out directions. Miller saw Morgan further along the corridor and he walked fast towards her.

'Morgan, what's going on?'

She looked at him. 'I'm sorry to tell you this, Frank, but Lizzie's dead.'

NINETEEN

'How's it going, mucker?' Calvin Stewart asked Finbar O'Toole. The smaller man was riffling through a cardboard box in his living room.

'Shite, but thanks for asking.'

'What are you greetin' over now?'

'I put my travel mug in one of these boxes and I can't find it.'

'What does it say on it? "Worst Treasure Hunter in the World"?'

'It's my steel one that keeps coffee hot for hours. I always take it in the car. Bastard thing.'

'This one here?' Stewart said, reaching into a box and pulling the mug out.

'Where did you find that?' Finbar asked suspiciously.

'Don't be saying it like I nicked the fucking thing and now I'm pretending to bring it back. It was in the box marked "kitchen". Where did you expect it to be? In a box labelled "useless fanny"?'

'Ha-ha. What are you doing round here in the middle of the day? Shouldn't you be packing?'

'I don't need to pack. All I need is my toothbrush and the clothes I'm standing in.'

'Manky bastard. How long have you been wearing those Y-fronts? Since Christmas Day?'

'For your information, I've delegated the packing to my daughter and the wee man. He's helping her, and right chuffed he is too that he's getting his grandpa's stuff together. I love that wee guy.'

Finbar looked at his friend. 'You left Carrie to do the packing? Bloody hell. Sexist bastard.'

'Hold your fucking horses there; she's just packing my clothes and my toiletries and some other crap I've got lying around. I'm leaving all the rest. But the flat I'm going to is a rental, and I'm renting my one out.'

'Harry McNeil's a good guy. That's not something you can say about most coppers.'

'Cheeky bastard. I've dug you out of a few scrapes.'

'I don't mean you, ya daft bastard. But Jimmy

Dunbar is a guy I would trust. You know, though, I have to say, if I had a friend who was a copper and I was in need, I know he would reach out and help me...'

'What are you havering about now? I'm the only copper friend you have.'

'That's good to know, because I'm in a sticky wicket.'

'What's up? You went to rub your arse cream on and you picked up the Deep Heat by mistake? Because if you have, there's no way I'm rubbing anything on your arse except a can of petrol and a box of matches.'

'Can you stop talking about arses for a minute? I'm in a pickle. You see, the selfish bastard who was supposed to move out of the flat I'm renting got a better job offer, so instead of moving to Inverness, he's staying put in Edinburgh, and the rental company isn't forcing him to move.'

Finbar stood looking at Stewart.

'And?' Stewart said.

Finbar smiled at him.

'Oh fuck, no,' Stewart said. 'There's no way you're moving in with me. Besides, you have Irene to think about.'

'Irene's a locum GP and she isn't moving right

away. Christ knows she moved down from Inverness to be with me in Glasgow, and now we're relocating again. So it was just going to be me moving through right now. Come on, Calvin. It's a two-bedroom flat you're moving into.'

'I don't care if it's Buckingham Palace. I need my own space.'

'You've not got a girlfriend at the moment. You'll just be sitting in your skids on the couch watching reruns of *Steptoe and Son*.'

'How do you know I haven't got a girlfriend?'

'Have you?'

Stewart hesitated. 'Not at the moment, but I've got my eye on somebody.'

'When is she due for release?'

Stewart shook his head. 'Just as well you're not the one who has to go into an interview room to try and get a killer to confess. He'd run rings round you.'

'Seriously though, pal. What am I going to do?'

'Call Harry McNeil. He has a big house. He'll let you stay with him.'

'I'm not going to ask Harry. That would be an imposition.'

'But you'll be quite happy farting and stinking my place out? And as much as I trust you, how do I know you won't go sleepwalking?'

'I don't sleepwalk.'

'How do I know?'

'Because I'm telling you. Irene would have told me if I'd done that.'

'Listen, Fin, I like you a lot, mate, but living with somebody is a whole new kettle of fish.'

'I'm not suggesting we get engaged. I mean, I'll have my own toothbrush.'

'Now you're just being a fucking weirdo.' Stewart followed his friend into the kitchen. Finbar put his mug on the counter, filled the kettle and switched it on.

'You want a coffee?' he asked Stewart.

'Aye, go on then. We found some bastard dumped in an industrial estate this morning and he's from Edinburgh. We have to find out why he was through there.'

'How did he die?'

'Stabbed.'

'At the scene?'

'Aye. There was a lot of blood. Fiona was there. She's doing the PM on him.'

'You think it was a drug deal gone bad or something?' Finbar put the coffee granules into two ordinary mugs, keeping his metal one for later.

'Could be. We're doing a background check on

him now. I want Jimmy and Evans to go through to Edinburgh. Lisa McDonald is taking charge at this end, under Lynn McKenzie.'

'While you three have a piss-up in Edinburgh?'

'Hardly a piss-up.' Stewart watched Finbar pour the coffees. 'You know, it's funny Jimmy being through there and I'll be the one staying behind when they come back through here.'

'Harry's crowd will keep you amused.'

'Aye, that they will. I'm glad Charlie Skellett is on the team. He and I worked together years ago and he's a good guy.'

Stewart got the milk from Finbar's fridge and poured some into each of the two mugs.

'What's that in your pocket?' Finbar asked Stewart as he eyed up the brightly coloured paper.

'Oh, this? I got this as a gift for your new job.' Stewart took it out and handed it over to Finbar.

'You shouldn't have,' he said, ripping the paper and taking the gift out. Finbar looked at it. 'No, really, you shouldn't have. What am I going to do with a stethoscope? I work on people after somebody wearing this pronounces them dead. Here, give it to the bairn to play with.'

He handed it back to Stewart, who shrugged and

put the medical instrument back in his pocket. 'Ungrateful bastard.'

'I know you meant well –'

'Shut up.'

'Listen, about the flat –'

'Fin, I'd love to, mate, but I'm seeing somebody. Nobody knows. And it's going to fucking stay that way.'

Finbar nodded. 'Okay. Why didn't you just say?'

'I'm not letting on.'

'Oh, right. So it's somebody we're not supposed to know about. It must be somebody we know.' He snapped his fingers and pointed to Stewart. 'It's Lisa McDonald!'

'Ya manky wee bastard. Don't ask me about it again.'

'It's fine. I've already booked a serviced apartment at Fountainbridge. I just thought if I could stay with you, I'd save money.'

'Listen to you. Save fucking money. If you were any tighter, your arse would squeak when you walked.'

'You can't blame a man for trying.'

'Keep that kind of talk for Irene.'

TWENTY

Harry walked into the hospital from the back car park, past an ambulance with its lights flashing and two patrol cars. Inside, the hospital felt stifling but not as claustrophobic as the mortuary was. He had quickly despatched Charlie Skellett and Lillian O'Shea to go down for Dale Wynn's postmortem. Charlie had asked if Harry was sure he didn't want to go down himself. Fuck that for a game of soldiers. If he wanted to smell something that would turn his stomach and make him toss his ring, he'd go and stand outside the sewage works.

There was a hive of activity in the hospital. More than usual. This place was relatively new and much more modern than the other buildings on the site, which might have been worthy of an award back when the mods were booting about on their scooters but were now a blight on the horizon.

Frank Miller was on the top floor, looking white, like he'd been stabbed and was losing all the blood in his system. He walked up to Harry as he approached.

'This is a fucking disaster,' he said.

'Take it easy, Frank and tell me what happened.' Harry quickly scanned the area for Morgan but didn't see her.

'Lizzie went to bed as usual, and everything was fine. She had pulled the covers up, so nothing seemed amiss until breakfast this morning. An orderly went in to get her and pulled back the covers and saw her face: no colour, eyes wide open.' Miller shook his head. 'I can't believe it.'

'Maybe things aren't what they seem.'

'You're thinking the same thing as me: she wanted to speak to me and now she's dead?'

'Exactly. But it's what we're paid to do, be suspicious. Where's Morgan? Have you spoken to her yet?'

Miller shook his head. 'She's busy dealing with things right now. Everybody is in an uproar. They're trying to calm down the patients now. They know something's going on and they're acting up.'

'I'm going to find her now and see exactly what happened.' Harry left Miller standing on his own. He passed a group of uniforms, a couple of whom he knew, and nodded to them.

He found Morgan standing talking to a uniformed inspector.

'Morning, sir,' the uniform said.

'Morning. I need to have a word with Dr Allan.'

'Certainly.' The inspector walked away to join the posse of uniforms and Harry turned to Morgan.

'I know you've spoken to the others, but can you tell me what happened?'

'Oh, Harry, this is awful. She was so young. It's heartbreaking. After all she went through!'

'I'm assuming a doctor pronounced her?' Harry asked.

'Yes. We have a couple of doctors here on site to deal with medications. One of them had a look but couldn't make any judgement on how she died. It could be a heart attack or any number of things.' She looked at him. 'Lizzie was young, but it's not unheard of.'

'I agree. We can't speculate. Has she had any visitors recently?'

'Her boyfriend, Ben, was here yesterday.'

'Was he left alone with her?'

Morgan shook her head. 'I was with him. She wouldn't talk to him. But even if he was in there without me, an orderly would have been with him. That's the rules. Only a lawyer would have been allowed private time, but he hasn't been around for ages.'

'Run me through the night's events.'

Morgan swallowed hard and Harry could see the emotion turmoil going on inside of her before she dug deep and her professionalism rose to the surface.

'It was a normal night. Nothing out of the ordinary. Lizzie went to bed, and she was found by the orderly this morning.'

'No offence, but we'll have to interview him and delve deep into his background.'

'I wouldn't expect anything less, Harry,' Morgan said.

'We're going to have to talk to her boyfriend as well. And anybody else who had contact with her.' He looked at her. 'Did she come into contact with any of the other patients?'

'They get to congregate for an hour or so. A few at a time, if they want to.'

'No other visitors?'

Morgan thought about it for a moment. 'Nobody else, except for Hamish.'

'Who's Hamish?'

'Hamish McKinley. He was a patient of mine. He's on the sex offenders register. He was urinating in the bushes one day near a picnic site and schoolkids were picnicking there, so he was arrested and charged with indecent exposure.'

'How did he know Lizzie?'

'She was an outpatient here too, remember? They got talking and they struck up a friendship. Hamish was here because he kept getting caught peeing outside and he wouldn't take a telling not to do it, but he said he had been under the doctor for a bladder problem, and this was confirmed. I think because he was on the register, he got picked up any time there was a paedophile suspected of something. Hamish's doctor arranged for him to come here. And I'm not breaking patient confidentiality; it's a matter of record and you can see that if you look him up.'

'And he spoke to Lizzie recently?'

'Last week he was here. I haven't seen him since.'

'Is he still a patient of yours?'

'Yes, he is.'

'How did an outpatient get to speak to Lizzie?'

'First of all, Harry, they were both outpatients at one time, so they knew each other. And secondly, Lizzie's boyfriend was an outsider, but with the proper authorisation he was allowed in. This is not a concentration camp.' Her breathing was getting heavier and her cheeks getting redder.

'Okay, I get it now.' He put a hand on her arm. 'This is an emotional time for everybody.'

'Her boyfriend lives in Glasgow. He comes through a few times a month to see if she'll speak to him.'

'I remember Ben. He seems like a nice guy.'

'He is. He thought the world of Lizzie.'

'I'll have to pay a visit to speak with Lizzie's stepmother.'

Morgan smiled at him. 'Still can't call her by her name, can you?'

Harry didn't answer right away, thinking that Morgan might be mocking him, but he saw in her eyes that she wasn't. 'You wouldn't happen to have Ben's contact number, would you?'

'I do. He's on a break from college just now, but I don't know what he's doing when he's not here. You can ask him.'

Harry wrote the number down in a notebook, then looked around. 'She'll have to be taken to the mortuary, but I don't think Kate will be allowed to touch her. Luckily, there's a new pathologist coming tomorrow. Finbar O'Toole.'

'I can't even imagine how Kate would be able to do the PM on Lizzie even if she was allowed to. Knowing what she did to Andy Watt.'

'I'll arrange to go to Saughton to speak to the mother.'

'Stepmother,' Morgan corrected. 'Lizzie never liked to call Maggie her mother.'

'I think she had quite a few names for Maggie, none of them charming.'

Professor Leo Chester, head pathologist at Edinburgh, came out of the room. It was protocol for a pathologist to attend when there was a sudden death at the hospital, as well as a doctor.

'No obvious signs just now,' he said. 'We'll know more when we have her on the table.'

'Thanks, Doc. I'll have a couple of my team come down tomorrow,' Harry said.

'Very good, Harry. See you then.'

The pathologist was looking old, kicking retirement age but hanging on by his fingertips.

A few minutes later, Lizzie's body was in a bag on a gurney being wheeled out along the corridor.

Harry looked at his watch, surprised to see how much time had passed. He was feeling hungry as it was approaching lunchtime, but eating would have to wait. He needed to go to Saughton Prison.

Then the phone rang.

'Hello?'

'Harry? It's Calvin Stewart again. I know you're aware I'm coming through to work with you all tomorrow, but we have a situation here – a murder to be exact. And the victim is from your end.'

'Do you have a name for him, sir?'

'Hamish McKinley. We're trying to establish what he was doing through here, but we need some-body in Edinburgh to go and knock on a door.'

'McKinley, you say?'

'Correct. We ran his name and he has form. Paedo, by all accounts.'

'Christ, we have a girl who's a sudden death at the psychiatric hospital here. And she had a visitor a few days ago.'

There was silence for a moment. *'Don't tell me it was this fucker McKinley?'*

'Sounds like the same one. I have a psychiatrist here who knows him. He was a patient of hers. We were just discussing him. It seems like he was caught when he was answering the call of nature, but they put him on the sex offenders register.'

'That's not what I hear, Harry, old son. Thing is, he was a kiddie fiddler. Nothing that could be proven, and he was always skating on thin ice, but nothing

ever stuck. It didn't stop your side bringing him in when there was something going on, but he always had an answer.'

'I wonder how Lizzie Armstrong got involved with him?'

'That's the case we worked on late last year? Her and her mother and that daft brother of Maggie Parks?'

'The very same. Lizzie was found dead this morning.'

'You might have led with that, Harry, son. Considering I'll be involved in it tomorrow.'

'Sorry, sir, it came as a bit of a shock.'

'Aye, well, never mind. You can catch me up when I come over. I appreciate you renting me that flat of yours. I won't forget that, son.'

'Only too glad to help out a colleague in need.'

'Aye, well, just be careful what one you choose to help. Some of these back-stabbing bastards are relentless. I've sent Jimmy and Robbie Evans through ahead of me, but something popped up about that bastard McKinley when I was having a wee look-see.'

'What was that, sir?'

'When McKinley was arrested, you were the arresting officer.'

TWENTY-ONE

'I swear to God, if you mention the words "magic" and "ball" in the one sentence again, I'll be spending my retirement in the Big Hoose.'

'Vern talks about it a lot nowadays. Ever since I moved in with her. She has a side to her that I didn't see before.'

'I bet she sees a side to *you* she never saw before.'

They were almost at Comely Bank, at the little hotel they stayed at when they were helping on a case over here.

'Like what?' Evans said, a worried look on his face.

'Like the way you sit around in your skids and vest on the weekends, watching cartoons.'

'How do you know I do that? Peeking through my windows?'

'You're not the only one who has a crystal ball.'

'I thought you said we're not allowed to use that term anymore?'

'I said *you* weren't, for fear of getting my boot up your jacksie,' Dunbar said. 'Besides, your maw called me before you took the leap and packed up all your porno mags to take to Vern's.'

'I don't need porno mags. I'm young and virile. I bet you have porno mags, though.'

'Cheeky bastard. I've had my fill of life, son. I'm happily married, and I'm sure Cathy would love it if I told her you said she was an old bag who was past satisfying her husband.'

'I never said that! You did.'

'That's what lies are for, to be embellished. She'll have your nuts in a vice. Plus, you'll be bumped for getting invited round at Christmas.'

'Och, away. I'll need to have a word with Cathy, tell her you must have had a stroke.' Evans drove through Comely Bank, past the Fettes station where they would be based. 'But what did my maw really say?'

'I don't know, she didn't call.' Dunbar grinned.

'Sake. But do you have an opinion about me being with Vern?'

'If she's into all this mumbo-jumbo shite, I would think twice about putting a ring on her finger until you find the real Vern. When you're living with her, the real one will show herself soon enough. There. That's my honest opinion.'

'Thanks, boss. Does that mean I'm back on the Christmas invite list?'

'Does it fuck.'

Evans parked up the car outside the hotel and they got out with their cases.

'Hard to believe that Calvin is going to be living permanently around the corner in Harry's flat,' Evans said.

'Better that than some arsehole who'll stop paying the rent.'

'Then it's a nightmare trying to get them out,' Evans said.

'If I had a place and that happened, I'd send round six guys I know with a van for a free removal. You think some dick would be sitting in my place living off me for free?'

Evans knew the person would be a real daftie to try such nonsense. There were laws, but they were made to be skirted.

They checked in and got back to the car and Evans drove back round to the Fettes station.

DI Frank Miller was standing at a whiteboard with Lillian O'Shea. DS Julie Stott was at her computer, as was Colin Presley. Charlie Skellett was noticeable by his absence.

'DCI Dunbar. Robbie,' Miller said. 'Good to see you again.'

'You too, son,' Dunbar said. 'Where's Harry?'

'He and Charlie are away up to Saughton to speak with Maggie Parks.'

'The death notice, so to speak.'

'Aye. More a courtesy, after what she did to the poor lassie.'

'I know she has to be told, but she held Lizzie captive,' Evans added. 'Then made her kill Andy Watt. That woman is pure evil. It's a wonder she wasn't the one in the psych hospital.'

'You said it yourself, Robbie,' Miller said. 'She's evil, not mental.'

'Aye, you're right,' Dunbar said. 'But Lizzie didn't know what she was doing.'

'We just need to know how she died. And something doesn't feel right about it. Not by a long shot,' Miller said.

TWENTY-TWO

Even with having to change at Stirling, the journey was very enjoyable. It had been a long time since Stacey Mitchell had been on a train.

She had a feeling Darren and Lesley might have cottoned on by now that she had taken off, but that was fine. If they had called ahead and a reception committee was waiting for her, they would be at Waverley. So she got off at Haymarket.

This was once recorded as the smelliest place in Edinburgh, but all she smelt was the warm air as she stepped onto a tram and took it along to Princes Street, her bag at her feet.

Her heart was racing now. She took out the piece of paper with the name written it on. Reading the name made it seem real.

There were so many more people walking in Princes Street than in the village where she lived, but she couldn't procrastinate. She had a job to do, and every time she thought of him, the anger intensified. Would she be able to control herself when the time came? She didn't know the answer to that.

Carrying her bag, she walked up Frederick Street and waited at the bus stop. She didn't have to wait long and then she was just an anonymous passenger, another face in a sea of faces. She sat at the back, looking out at the passing shops, and bided her time until it was her stop.

Harry McNeil's flat was just around the corner. Her anger was starting to get the better of her, but she controlled it. Stacey had been good at doing that for a long time now.

Stacey felt her stomach rumble, but she couldn't eat or else she would be sick. There was a Co-op opposite the bus stop, so it would be easy enough to pop in there before she did what she was about to do. No. What if she was sick? In *there*. Where she was going. That wouldn't do at all.

Stacey got off the bus and walked along the main road, heading towards Broughton High School, but that wasn't where she was going, of course. She turned left into Comely Bank Place and walked round until she saw the Dean Bowling Club. She knew she was in the right place.

She stood at the side of the tall hedge surrounding the club and looked up at the stone building opposite. Then she put her head down, keeping a firm grip on her bag. She was sweating now and she wished she had put shorts on, but this was Scotland, so jeans it was.

Of course, she had packed a couple of light jackets in her bag and an umbrella.

Then she was across to the stair entrance and she was in. Up to the top floor, and this was where it was going to be tricky. If the next-door neighbour came out and saw what she was doing, then it might be all over and then she would have to let the deck fall.

She put the bag down and took the little lock-picking set out of her pocket. She slipped a pick into the lock, feeling for the tumblers. And that's when she heard the stair door open again and feet starting to climb the stone steps. Stacey knew then that if she tried to hurry too much, she would panic, and if the feet were coming up here, she would have a hard time explaining away her presence.

She tuned everything out and concentrated, and then the lock turned and she turned the handle, standing up and grabbing her bag. She closed the door as if there was a bomb attached to it and slamming it would set it off.

The feet kept coming up and then McNeil's neighbour was in and Stacey heard the door close.

The next hurdle would be if there was anybody inside. She looked at her watch: mid-afternoon. There shouldn't be anywhere here, but you never knew. So she suddenly moved fast, checking the bedrooms before moving into the living room and the kitchen off it.

Nothing. It was empty. She had been prepared to fight, but she would only be fighting with her own shadow.

McNeil wasn't here. Never mind.

She looked around, at a dresser that sat against one wall. It had some framed photos on it, and one was of a smiling man and woman. It was what was on the woman's face that shot anger through her. Somebody had taken the photo out and drawn an X over each of the woman's eyes.

Stacey picked the frame up and smacked it against the side of the unit, smashing it. She looked at the broken glass on the floor, then immediately regretted her actions. She found a little brush and dustpan and swept it up, then got the vacuum cleaner and ran it over the carpet.

Some of the pieces were still around the inside edge of the frame and she thought about taking them out, but she decided to leave them.

She walked back through to the main bedroom and opened the wardrobe door. There were some women's clothes hanging there. Not a lot; maybe she only stayed over on the weekend.

She closed the wardrobe door, feeling the anger welling up again. She hadn't taken her meds recently and was starting to feel sick. She hadn't eaten for hours, so maybe that was it.

She went into the kitchen and opened the fridge door, looking inside while she kept hold of the handle. There was very little inside except for some individually wrapped cheese slices. She took a couple, unwrapped them and ate them, tossing the wrappers in the bin.

She lifted a kitchen knife from the block sitting on the countertop and made slashing motions through the air with it before putting it back.

After sitting down on the couch and looking at the TV without switching it on, she decided enough was enough. How long was she going to wait here for anyway?

It was at this point that the doubt crept in.

And that was when she heard the key being put in the lock.

She jumped up as quietly as she could and stood like a deer in the headlights. The door opened and she was about to blurt something out when a young woman walked in with a little boy. She was carrying a couple of grocery bags.

She jumped for a second. 'Oh, sorry. I was told this place would be vacated by today. I can come back.'

'No, it's fine,' Stacey said, smiling at the boy, who smiled back.

'I'm Carrie Stewart and this is my son, Eddie. Say hello to the nice lady.'

'Hello.'

'Hello. My name's Stacey.' The boy wasn't shy, but he wasn't overly rambunctious either. Well-rounded, she thought.

'I didn't realise Harry would have somebody waiting,' Carrie said.

'Last-minute thing.'

'I'm not the one moving in. It's my dad. We're from Glasgow, but work is bringing him through here,' Carrie explained.

'Oh, right. I wasn't sure when I saw you,' Stacey said, winging it.

'I just wanted to put some groceries in the fridge for my dad. He won't have time tomorrow.'

'That's very nice of you,' Stacey said.

'Harry said he would have the flat checked over before my dad moves in, just to make sure everything is in working order.'

'It is. I just finished checking.'

'You want to stay for a cuppa?'

Stacey hesitated, before shaking her head. 'No, thanks. I still have work to do.'

'Okay. It was nice meeting you, Stacey.'

'You too, Carrie.'

Stacey walked out of the flat and back down the stone steps to the bottom, then back out into the sunshine.

Then the panic hit her like a sledgehammer. What had she done, coming here? Her anger had blinded her. Tears filled her eyes. This had been foolhardy.

She reached into her bag and pulled out the small mobile phone and turned it on.

'It's me,' she said when it was answered at the other end. She told him her location and was told to stay where she was.

Ten minutes later, a car pulled up. A black BMW with blacked-out windows. She hurried over, opened the back door and slipped in. The driver said nothing as he drove away. Stacey looked out of the window up to Harry McNeil's flat one more time before the car turned the corner and it was out of sight.

TWENTY-THREE

Back then

It was dark and the streetlights did little to dispel the sense of dread that he was feeling. The doctor felt his legs shaking and he thought he was going to be sick, but he stood his ground. This had to end. Nothing had been done, not to his satisfaction. The police had given him all the drivel about justice, but justice hadn't been served. *He had an alibi,* they said. The Crown Office had to drop the case against the man and instructed the police to carry on with their investigation.

Of course, they came up with nothing. Why

would they? The murdering bastard had got away with it. How many times had he got away with stuff before? He'd been cautioned before for standing near a playground acting suspiciously, but he'd never been arrested. The police recognised him in the photo at Cramond, but they couldn't prove anything. This monster was allowed to walk free while his little boy was dead. Life wasn't fair, but tonight he was going to change things.

In his backpack was a machete. He would make McArthur squeal like the pig he was.

The doctor was waiting a little bit down the road from where McArthur lived in Barnton. Lived with his mum and dad, because he was too fucking lazy to get a job himself.

He was about to jump the garden wall and break into McArthur's house when he sensed somebody behind him. He gasped and pulled out the home-made blackjack that he was going to hit MacArthur with, thinking it was the young man himself standing behind him.

'You're going about it all the wrong way,' the patient said. Of course, he wasn't a patient at the time, but he would be one day.

'What?' the doctor said.

'I said, you're going about it all the wrong way. I've been watching you. I wondered when you would try something like this. I don't want you throwing your life away.'

Adrenaline was flowing through the doctor's heart now. What should he do? Smack this man and run? No, that wouldn't be the smartest thing he'd ever done. Neither was murdering somebody, but even that wasn't as bad as hitting this man.

'My life is already over. My boy is dead, so what's the point in me living?'

'If you kill Tommy McArthur tonight, you'll be in jail in a few hours. If you want to kill him, you have to be smart about it.'

The doctor stood looking at the man, not quite sure what was going on. He didn't know what to say next.

'If you want to kill him, then let's leave. I'll show you how to do it without getting caught.'

The doctor thought it was a joke at first, but then saw the man was deadly serious. 'Why? Why would you do this for me?'

'Tommy McArthur has always been one step in front of the law. That alibi he was given was a sham. His friend is a registered sex offender. He exposed himself in public, pretending it was only public urination. But McArthur, he's a whole different animal. He's tried to take little boys before, but never succeeded. He was given a caution before, and that's what landed him on the register. That's what drew attention to him. Everybody knows he's guilty. And if you kill him tonight, you'll have taken care of him, but then you'll be put away with the other animals in their cages.' The man shook his head. 'You don't want that. You wouldn't survive one minute. However, if you're smart about it, you can do it and nobody will ever be able to prove a thing. You'll have an alibi: me. I'll show you how to take care of him without you getting caught.'

'You want him dead too?'

'It's the only way to get rid of scum like him. His friend will still be walking about, but at least this beast will never do to another little boy what he did to Cormack. Just think about it for a second. You can climb that garden wall, or you can come with me. I'm not going to force you. This will have to be your decision.'

'And you'll teach me?'

'I will. I promise you we'll never get caught.'

Three weeks later, Tommy McArthur's body

was found hanging in the woods. The official cause of death was listed as suicide.

And nobody thought any different. Except for his parents, who were adamant that he wouldn't have committed suicide. Nobody listened. Nobody cared.

And nobody was ever caught.

TWENTY-FOUR

Now

'Been a long time since I was here,' DI Charlie Skellett said, looking up at the exterior of Saughton Prison. It was officially called HMP Edinburgh, but Harry had never heard it be called by its proper name.

'Me too,' Harry said. 'I've put a lot of these bastards away in here.'

'Can imagine you being sentenced and put in here with them?'

'Not really. I'd be stuck in my own cell for twenty-three hours a day.'

'I hope this bitch we're going to see is bored off her tits,' Skellett said as they were led inside.

After all the rigmarole, they were shown into a room to wait for their guest, who appeared five minutes later, all smiles.

'This is a nice surprise, Harry,' Maggie Parks said. Harry noticed the woman had lost weight, but he didn't want to mention it in case she took it the wrong way, like he was trying it on with her, giving her a compliment.

She was the one responsible for murdering her live-in partner, DCI Paddy Gibb. One of them. She had been one of them too.

'We're not here with a bunch of flowers and a box of chocolates,' Skellett said.

Her smiled left her face. 'I sort of remember you. Always a weedy little fucker, weren't you? Had an eye for the ladies. Used to perv yourself around the younger female uniforms. Charlie fucking Skellett. I never thought I'd see the day you'd be sitting in here unless it was in a different kind of uniform.'

Skellett smiled. 'Nice try, sweetheart, but it's going to take a far more intelligent creature than you to rattle my chains. I've been around the block a few times. You used to pick up wee bits of blood and what have you from crime scenes, but me and Harry? We've sat across from a lot more smarter bastards than you. So go ahead, try your wee psychology rants.'

Maggie Parks smiled at Harry. 'Worth a try. You got any cigarettes?'

Harry looked her in the eyes and thought that if he did have any cigarettes, he would stub one out on her eyeball.

'You know I don't smoke.'

'Paddy smoked. I always said that the cigarettes would kill him, but there it was; I'm the one who killed him instead. A good shove down the stone steps at the flat, and even then he didn't die right away.' The smile danced on her lips, as if remembering that night around seven months prior was giving her a thrill. Harry seriously began to question Maggie's sanity and thought that maybe she should have been locked away in the psychiatric hospital next to her stepdaughter.

'I want to talk to you about something,' Harry said.

'Why? I already confessed. It's only cowards and the weak-minded who lie and try to get out of it. I killed Paddy. There. My lawyer said I shouldn't say stuff like this, but who cares? It's not as if I'm ever going to walk out of here.'

Harry gave a short laugh. 'You're throwing your chance away to try and prove you're innocent.'

'I'm not innocent. You told me I threw Paddy down the stairs, and that's what I believe because I can't remember what went on back then. Therefore, I'm guilty.'

God, she was good. Coming right out and admitting she was a murderer, then twisting things around so she could later say in court that she didn't know what she was saying. Maybe her angle was getting a doctor to say she was incompetent to stand trial, just like her stepdaughter.

'I have to admit it was a nice touch, sending your stepdaughter round to harm me and my baby,' Harry said, and the thought of that day made his blood boil.

'Still trotting this one out, are we? Dear oh dear, you must be desperate. Hasn't Lizzie told you why she did it?'

'She's not going to tell us why.'

'Then that's her prerogative.'

'That's not why she can't tell us,' Skellett said.

'Oh? And what would stop her telling you? Oh, wait, she's in a mental ward.' Maggie sat back and laughed.

'She's dead,' Harry said, unable to listen to the laughing anymore.

Maggie stopped like she had been slapped in the face. 'What do you mean, she's dead?'

'Life extinct,' Skellett said. 'You're familiar with the term, aren't you? You've been at enough crime scenes.'

'Don't be a smartarse, Skellett, it doesn't suit you.' There was a crack in the veneer now and Harry knew they had got through to her.

'She was found dead in her room this morning in the hospital,' Harry said.

Silence hung in the air between them while Maggie processed this.

'How?' was all she said.

'There were no obvious signs of trauma, nothing outward, so she's been taken down to the Cowgate for her PM. It's scheduled for tomorrow.'

'She didn't have any underlying medical conditions,' Maggie said. 'What the hell happened?'

'We don't know yet,' Harry said. Then he looked Maggie in the eyes. 'You seem to be so concerned for your stepdaughter, yet you set her up for a fall, using her phone to send Andy Watt a text so you could run him down. Then you had her finish the job when you didn't kill him. I hope you're proud of yourself. Andy's dead now, run over by Lizzie.'

'It wasn't Lizzie.'

'Of course it was. She killed Andy, then she came to my house and tried to kill the babysitter. And my fucking daughter.' Harry realised he was starting to lose it, so he reined himself back in.

'I heard about that. I don't know why she would want to do that. Something doesn't sit right with that. Why would she be at your house? With a knife?'

'Because you told her to. You fed Lizzie lies for years, making her psychotic. Lizzie told Morgan about it. What's the point in denying it?'

'It's the truth,' Maggie said. 'No, I wasn't feeding Lizzie lies for years, and she wasn't involved in any of this stuff. I used her to throw you off the trail, but she isn't a killer.'

'She reversed over Andy in a van and killed him.'

'She wouldn't have done that.'

'She killed Andy and she came to my house looking for me. There's no denying she was there. I came in after she attacked my girlfriend and my baby daughter. There's nothing you can say that will change that.'

Maggie looked at him. 'How do you know she killed Andy Watt? Do you have any witnesses? You found the van burned out, completely. You have nothing to prove she killed Andy.'

'You would have been able to tell her how to destroy evidence, how to burn the van so there was no DNA, no prints.'

'I would have. But I didn't.'

Harry shook his head. 'Why protect Lizzie? She was your stepdaughter, not your flesh and blood.'

'She was like my flesh and blood. And I'm not protecting her. I already told you I killed Paddy. Why would I lie about Lizzie? But you go right ahead and keep on thinking that way, Harry. She's dead, and now the real killer is still walking about free, laughing behind your back. He'll have got away with it, and he'll be delighted. He's pulled the wool over your eyes. And you'll sleep at night knowing that Lizzie is dead, that she won't be able to come back and have another go at you and your baby, but the bastard who put the idea into her head is still walking about. What's to stop *him* coming back and having another go? And finishing the job this time? You think about that, Harry McNeil. You're a smart man. If Lizzie is dead, then somebody took her life. She didn't die of natural causes.'

Her breathing was heavy now as she was getting ramped up. 'Now I'm going back to my cell. But hear this: you can never say you weren't warned. And you're a witness to this, Skellett. Don't come running to me, Harry McNeil, when somebody tries to kill you. But if I'm wrong about Lizzie, then you can feel free to let me know.'

And with that, the interview was over.

TWENTY-FIVE

Jimmy Dunbar pulled into the side of the road as Robbie Evans looked at the door numbers.

'There it is, number sixty-eight, ground-floor flat,' he said.

'Nice wee place,' Dunbar said, turning off the engine. 'I wonder if the neighbours know about McKinley being a paedo?'

'I doubt it. A lot of them look just like you and... well, just you,' Evans added.

'Cheeky bastard.'

'No offence boss, but sometimes you wear that scabby old mac in the winter and it makes you look like you wear it in the pictures.'

'Get out the car before I set fire to you. Bloody

mac. It's a raincoat, and just because it doesn't have a stupid fucking logo on it, doesn't make it any less effective against the elements. In fact, it's probably better made than that designer shite you wear.' Dunbar slammed the door.

'I was just observing, boss.'

'Observe this.' Dunbar stuck two fingers up at Evans.

'Being childish now,' Evans said in a low voice as he made his way along the path to the front door, Dunbar close behind.

The door opened fast before they got there and an old woman with no top teeth and wearing an apron stood there looking for a fight.

'And you lot can fuck right off. He's no' here.'

'Well, that clears up the mess of the missing Santa Claus,' Dunbar said, 'but we'd like to speak to the resident.'

'Oh, you're funny, son. I'll give you Santa Claus in a minute.'

'Listen, we need to speak to somebody at this address who knows Hamish McKinley. I'm DCI Dunbar and this is my colleague DS Evans. Glasgow division.'

There was a subtle shift in the woman's

demeanour, noticed by both detectives, at the mention of McKinley.

'I'm his grandmother, Eileen McKinley. What do you want with him?'

'We'd really like to do this inside,' Dunbar said, his voice softer now, remembering why they were here in the first place.

Granny looked both ways before stepping back. 'Hurry up then, before that nosy old cow down the road sees you. It's bad enough that they spread rumours about Hamish that aren't true. According to legend, he stalks the streets at night with a hammer, preying on the elderly and young women. They all shite themselves. Needless to say, none of the wee bastards round here give me any lip.'

The two detectives stepped over the threshold and went into the house. It smelled stale, like the chip pan had been going full tilt but no window had been open to let the smell out.

'Through the back on the right,' she said, and the two men went into the living room.

'You've got to understand, Hamish has the mental age of a boy. Whatever he does wrong, he doesn't mean it. And when he had his pants round his knees in the public toilets in front of those boys, that's just the way he pees.'

The living room looked like a hovel, with furniture that would have looked right at home on top of a bonfire. Dunbar thought that it might be worth a lot of money in a few years as a collectible, but right now it had Guy Fawkes night written all over it.

'We've been sent to talk about Hamish,' Dunbar said.

'Look, he wanders about all day doing God knows what. But he stays out of trouble. I only worry about what will happen to him when I pop my clogs.'

'Please take a seat, Mrs McKinley,' Dunbar said.

She sat down and looked at him. 'What's wrong, son? Has Hamish got himself into trouble again?'

'I'm sorry to tell you this, but your grandson is dead.'

Mrs McKinley put a hand to her chest and sat back in the chair, making it creak alarmingly. 'Jesus, no. Oh, please no. Not my wee boy. Please no. I couldn't take it if he was deid.'

'I'm really sorry,' Evans said.

Then Mrs McKinley sat up as if she'd just been given a jolt of electricity from the chair. 'Sorry? You bastards hounded him all the time. Never let up. Always thought he was pulling his willy out in public.'

'To be fair, he was arrested four times for indecent exposure,' Dunbar said.

'He had a weak bladder! Sometimes he had to go for a pish in the bushes or else he would pish himself. Who wants to go about looking like that? But that wasn't good enough for the courts. Made him out to be a pervert.'

'He was arrested for having his trousers round his ankles in a public toilet,' Dunbar added.

'There was no paper in the cubicle. He just got caught short.'

Dunbar sensed that they were going round in circles and quickly moved on, cursing himself for listening to Evans and not having a FLO with them.

'Regardless of what went on in the past, I have to say that somebody murdered him in Glasgow.'

Again, the hand on the chest. 'Jesus and Mary. My poor boy. Why would anybody want to kill him?'

Dunbar saw Evans's brow furrow and thought the younger detective was going to blurt out, 'Because he was a paedo', so he slightly shook his head while the old woman's eyes rolled about in her head.

'That's what we're trying to find out.'

It was as if the director shouted 'Cut!' and she stopped her wailing. 'But you won't, will you? Find out, I mean. My Hamish is dead and it'll be swept under the carpet.'

'No, it won't,' Dunbar assured her. 'But you have to help us. And you can start by telling us what he was doing in Glasgow.'

TWENTY-SIX

'It's been a long day,' Lynn McKenzie said, pouring two glasses of wine.

'It has that,' Calvin Stewart said, stretching his legs out. 'Cheers.' He took a glass from Lynn and she sat down beside him on the couch. They clinked glasses.

'This is just typical,' she said. 'We're getting on better than we ever did, and you're moving away tomorrow.' She put a hand on his leg.

'Some long-distance relationships don't last, but I'm only going to be an hour away along the motorway.'

'Oh, Calvin, I'll wait for you no matter how long you're away,' Lynn replied in her best dramatic voice.

'Just as well you're a copper, because I don't think the stage is your next career move.'

She laughed and leaned over to kiss him. 'I know we weren't going to talk shop, but did Jimmy get back to you about our victim? I mean, we know his background, but did they find out why he was through in Glasgow?'

'His grandmother says he was through visiting a friend. They met online playing video games, if you can believe that,' Stewart said.

'And let me guess: this friend doesn't exist?'

'Correct. So what the hell was he doing through here? He didn't work, didn't have a girlfriend that we know of.'

'Maybe he was up to his old tricks,' Lynn said. 'But he was branching out because Edinburgh would be on to him.'

'The bag of pills that forensics found in his pocket worries me,' Stewart said. 'I had one of my pals from the drugs squad have a look and he reckons fentanyl. We won't be sure until we get them tested, but that won't take long.'

'I'm curious to find out what killed Lizzie Armstrong. A young, fit twenty-something. No obvious signs of trauma.'

'Call me old-fashioned,' Stewart said, 'but it's the

old saying: we don't believe in coincidences. It just so happens that Hamish McKinley was there visiting her last week, and then he's murdered, with fentanyl found in his pockets. Then she dies with no obvious cause.'

'You're thinking overdose?' Lynn put her wine glass on the coffee table.

'I am. I can't help it. It's the copper in me. I mean, I might be way off, and I hope it was something like a heart attack or something equally mundane so we can take anything else off the table, but what if McKinley gave her something?'

'There's always an orderly there when there's a visitor, isn't there?'

'Yes. That's the only fly in the ointment. Maybe I'll have Harry go and question the bloke if anything comes back from the PM toxicology. Also, I think we need to interview this Tasker guy, the boyfriend. He was round at the hospital a lot, but he wasn't at the hospital when they found Lizzie. He's not been answering his phone either. You could have Lisa McDonald go round to his flat, but not on her own. There's some new ginger-heid in MIT now. Get him to go along. Then you can see if he's worth his salt. Or at the very least, he can be cannon fodder.'

'Jesus, Calvin, ginger-heid?'

'You know what I'm like. Everybody's an arse-hole until they prove otherwise.'

'I'm starting to think along those lines too.'

TWENTY-SEVEN

Back then

'I feel like shit,' the patient said.

'That's because you're dying, remember?' the doctor said. 'Six to twelve months, I said.'

'When you stop giving me whatever it is that makes me look like a sick hundred-year-old man, then I intend to live a full life, Doc.'

'I'm going to give you a course of drugs that will start to counteract the effects of the drugs I gave you. It's going to take a little while to reverse it. A nurse will come in and she'll have to see you sick, then it's up to you whether you want her back. Tell her you're going to live in Cornwall, if you like. Or Golspie.

She'll visit you once, which will be tomorrow, then it's up to you. She won't question it.'

The doctor took a syringe out and held it up, squirting some of the liquid into the air.

'You know,' the patient said, 'you could be giving me liquid vitamins for all I know. You could let me die and then you'd be free and clear. You got your revenge and you could walk away.'

'First of all, I wouldn't do that. I'm a man of my word. Plus, you're going to help me with that other project, you said.'

The patient grinned and then coughed. 'I am. And I'm looking forward to it.'

'So am I.' The doctor's eyes glazed over for a moment. His mind was elsewhere, going back years. It had been a long time since he'd thought about Cormack, and he felt guilty every time he did think of his son and realised how long it had been.

The patient was lying in bed, his face gaunt, his eyes red. If he hadn't known better, the doctor would have thought this man really did only have a few months left to live. He put the needle in the man's arm and pressed the plunger. This was going to take a little time, but the patient would be back on his feet in no time and the first part of their plan would be finished. Then it would be on to stage two.

'Are you comfortable here? In this flat?'

'I am. It's not being used just now and nobody will question it. I have a lot of friends, Doctor, and one of them very kindly found this place for me. The owner won't be back for a while.'

'That's good. You rest now, and I'll have some-body come in and check on you later, then I'll be back. You're on the uphill road to recovery now.'

The patient smiled. 'Thanks, Doc. I promise you you're going to feel even better than you did the first time when we hanged that bastard. This is going to be up close and personal.'

The doctor smiled. This was going against every-thing he stood for, the Hippocratic Oath, everything. But he didn't care. When he was on his knees in front of his little boy's grave, he shed tears of sorrow and anger, thinking he would never get the chance to make the hurt go away. And this was certainly help-ing. He would go soon and see his little boy. He would tell him what his daddy was doing to punish the bad men who'd hurt him.

And how his friend was going to help him.

TWENTY-EIGHT

Now

Harry McNeil liked the Merlin in Morningside. It reminded him of how Morgan Allan had come into his life.

He'd had to attend mandatory therapy after his sabbatical, where he'd bought a house down in the south of Scotland, telling himself he would never go back to Edinburgh. His wife dying had hit him hard and he knew his baby daughter was in good hands with Alex's sister, Jessica. But circumstances had intervened and he had ended up coming back into Grace's life. His therapy had been with Dr Burke but the old guy was retired now. Sometimes Harry would skip the session and go straight to the bar. Morgan used to come in after work on a Friday and they had got talking. He had felt more comfortable talking to her in the bar than he had done with the old doctor.

After what had happened today with Lizzie dying, he thought Morgan might have enjoyed coming up here for a swift one before she went home. She had readily agreed.

Now here he was, sitting waiting for her. There was a young crowd in. It wasn't as busy as it would be the following night, Friday, but busy enough. He looked at his watch; she was ten minutes late. Never mind, it had been a long day for both of them. She hadn't wanted to come along to his place for a bite to eat, and of course he hadn't been invited to hers. They'd known each other for eight or nine months and had been dating for six, but he had only set foot in her house once.

The ghost of David still lingered, she had told him – he was hoping she had meant metaphorically – and he had respected her decision. She had also said that she felt more comfortable coming round to his place because he had Grace. He told her that

Jessica looked after Grace and it wouldn't be a problem for him to stay over at Morgan's place, but she had told him she didn't feel comfortable with that. A woman living on her own having a man stay over. She'd had a brief fling with a man years ago and they'd had a falling out while he had been staying over and she'd felt threatened in her own home.

Harry didn't push the matter. The last thing he wanted was for Morgan to think he was some nut job.

He looked at his watch again. He'd called Jimmy Dunbar earlier and told him if he didn't make it for a pint tonight then he would definitely catch up tomorrow. Jimmy had told him not to worry about it but to be aware that Stewart was coming through to live in Edinburgh the following day and would probably want to tag along. It wouldn't be a problem if Stewart was there, Harry had told him.

The door opened and Morgan walked in and Harry's heart skipped a beat for a second. To say he was pleased to see her was an understatement.

'Hi, honey. Sorry I'm late,' she said, coming over. She looked tired.

'I thought you might like to unwind with a couple before you go home,' Harry said.

'Thank you.'

The barman came over with Morgan's first drink and another beer for Harry.

'This was quite a shock today,' she said, clinking glasses with Harry. 'I can't believe Lizzie's gone.'

'I know. That girl has been through some tough shit this past six months.'

'Tell me about it. She killed Andy Watt, then tried to kill me and the baby. I don't know what was going through her mind.' She sat on the bar stool next to him. 'I mean, when she was rescued after being held captive by her stepmother, that was bad enough. She wouldn't open up and I knew this was going to be a long road we were going down.'

'Why do you think she wanted to talk to Frank?'

'I don't know. Maybe her visit from Hamish had sparked something inside her. She always liked him.'

'Did she know the real Hamish?' Harry asked, sipping his pint. 'You know, Morgan, that he was a paedophile.'

'Oh, Harry, you know I can't talk about a patient like that.'

'Let me talk about him, then, from a copper's point of view: he was arrested several times for exposing himself in public toilets to kids. He said he was just trying to find toilet paper. He was ordered to get help after his last bout of flashing to prevent him going to prison and he was sent to you.'

'If you say so.' She drank some of her vodka.

'I do. But now I'm wondering if he started some nonsense with Lizzie. They got on together, you said, because they were both outpatients. But what if he started something and that something triggered some memory inside Lizzie's head?'

'I can't say for sure if anything happened. She was allowed visitors, just like a prisoner without mental health issues would be allowed a visitor, so they spoke several times. I wasn't privy to what they discussed, only if Lizzie wanted to tell me, which she didn't,' Morgan said.

'Look, I didn't ask you to come here so I could grill you about McKinley, but I've known Lizzie for a long time. I first met her when she was a teenager. I didn't know her as well as Frank, obviously, but I remember her as a bright young girl, keen to get on in life. Paddy adored her like a real daughter, even though he had his own.'

'She was taken too soon. Her stepmother got into her head and twisted it.'

'Her step-grandfather was a serial killer. And now her mother is a killer too. One is long dead, and one is rotting away for the rest of her life,' Harry said.

'She never had a chance, did she, Harry?'

'Not at all. The odds were stacked against her. I'd like a word with her boyfriend, Ben. Do you know if he went back to their flat in Glasgow?'

'I assume. He was cut up about it when I told him. I said if he ever needs to talk, then he can come and talk to me.'

'Some of my colleagues will want to talk to him tomorrow.'

'Go easy on him, Harry. He's still in shock.'

'We will. Did Lizzie have any personal effects? I don't know where they would go to, mind.'

'She has nothing. Just a bunch of drawings. She drew on a pad, but we could only give her crayons. It kept her amused, though, and she seemed to enjoy it.'

Harry could see tears welling in Morgan's eyes.

'I thought we could help her,' Morgan went on, 'but that stepmother of hers really got into her head. I wish Lizzie would have spoken to me, but I knew it could take years for her to get comfortable talking.'

'We still have the recordings from when we interviewed her,' Harry said. 'She was a lot more talkative then, but it was mostly rambling. I talked to her about being held captive by her mother in the church and she spoke freely about that. But even the mention of Maggie's name made her cringe and pull her knees up to her chest.'

'She spoke back then?' Morgan looked surprised. 'You never mentioned that.'

'We had to interview her, Morgan. Whether she spoke or not, we had to talk to her.'

'Was her lawyer present?'

'She didn't want one, and as you know, we can't force her to have one present. In fact, she was adamant that she would only speak to us. But later on she was given a lawyer just to keep everything straight, and that was when she was deemed unfit to stand trial.'

'I feel so bad for her. Maggie has a lot to answer for.'

Harry didn't tell Morgan of the conversation he'd had with Lizzie's stepmother earlier that day.

'Now, are you hungry?' he said.

'It doesn't seem right, us going out like this.'

'We're not celebrating. Just going for a bite to eat.'

'Okay, sure. Where do you want to go?'

'Your choice.'

She knew of a nice little place just down the road

in Bruntsfield. Harry hid his disappointment well. He was hoping she'd say her place. Not tonight.

They finished their drinks and left, but Harry's mind wasn't on Morgan. It was on a young woman who couldn't speak up for herself anymore, and Harry still had a lot of questions for her.

TWENTY-NINE

Stacey Mitchell stood and looked out of the kitchen window in the darkness. There were lights in the distance. She wondered if they were from some house where the people lived a normal life. People who were happy and sad together, who woke up beside each other every morning and who shared the joys of life together.

Not like her. Going to bed alone, waking up alone. Yes, she had company, but it wasn't the same.

She'd come back here in the BMW. Driven right to the door by a friend of a friend.

She'd thought that Darren would lecture her, but he was so sweet about it. She loved him for that. And Lesley too. She had been concerned. Stacey had apologised to them both and promised she wouldn't go off like that again. But it was hard.

She took the piece of paper out of her pocket and looked at the name again for the millionth time.

Harry McNeil.

Her anger spread like wildfire throughout her whole body. One day she would come face to face with him. That was a given. It was the waiting that was killing her.

But she had time on her hands. She would wait.

She just hoped that it wasn't too late by then.

THIRTY

Harry paid for their dinner, at a little bistro in Bruntsfield, near the Links.

'I read about that councillor being stabbed to death,' Morgan said. 'It makes you feel like you can't walk anywhere at night alone. Even when there are a lot of people going about. All the visitors and locals.'

'It can happen anywhere,' he said, as they walked down to the main road, where their cars were parked.

'So, night cap at your place?' he said, trying once more.

'Oh, Harry, you know how I feel about that. Please have patience. I'm going to sell the house and move into somewhere smaller. It was David's idea to buy that big pile, and it was a great investment, but now I just rattle about in it. To be honest, I hate the place now. I even think it's haunted. It's so old, I'm sure somebody died in it at some stage of its life. Plus, it has bittersweet memories, what with David cheating on me and then coming home and pretending everything was okay. It's had its good times, but in the last ten years, it's had bad times too.'

'I understand,' Harry said, but he didn't. A house was bricks and mortar. You made the memories in a house. His girlfriend Vanessa had died in the house that she had left to him, the one in Murrayfield. He didn't dwell on the fact.

'We could have gone to your house, but the live-in nursemaid will be there.'

'We've been over this; Jessica is my sister-in-law, nothing more.'

'Ex sister-in-law. And I don't think she likes me being there. Every time I'm over, I'm always made to feel like I shouldn't be there. But as a psychiatrist, I deal with it. The problem's hers, not mine.'

Harry used a little bit of psychology himself and didn't tell her that it was all in her mind. 'Jessica's staying over at her friend's house this weekend,' he said instead.

Morgan smiled. 'That's terrific. I can come over tomorrow evening after work, then we can have a lot of fun.'

'I can't wait.' He put his hand on her waist and kissed her. Then she pulled back.

'Sorry. I don't want to start something we can't finish.'

He laughed and she unlocked her car.

'Take care. I'll call you tomorrow.'

He watched her get in the car and take off, honking the horn as she went, which was a pet peeve of his. *I've just said goodbye. I don't need you to re-enact some road-rage scenario.*

He walked to his own car. A bus passed going down Bruntsfield and he looked across at it. A man wearing a straw hat and sunglasses looked across at Harry from his seat on board. At Harry or at the people enjoying the late-evening sun on the Links?

The face looked familiar, Harry thought. But this man had a dark-coloured goatee. No, it was one of those déjà vu moments.

He got in the car and took his phone out and stuck it on the little holder on the dash. He'd turned the sound off and saw now that he had missed a text message from somebody. Benny. Who the hell was Benny?

Chance, his son, was always telling him he should get an Apple watch with cellular instead of wearing some cheap traditional watch, but he hated the idea of being on an electronic leash.

He saw he had missed a call too. Which wasn't good news when you were a murder squad detective.

'Crap,' he said and grabbed the phone again. He started the car as he listened to the message.

'DI McNeil. Sorry to bother you. A while back you said if I ever needed anything, I could call you. So here I am. I collected Lizzie's things today because she was my girlfriend, and her stepmother is...away. It's mostly drawings she did in crayon. I looked at them and I started crying. Listen, I know you think she killed Andy Watt, but she told me she didn't. I believe her. She thought they were listening to her every word at the hospital, because she had said something to me before and they ended up confiscating something. I can't remember. Can you give me a call? Cheers.'

Harry cut the call and dialled the number and Ben Tasker answered almost right away.

'It's Harry McNeil, Ben. You left a message.'

'Thanks for calling. I didn't know what else to do.'

'Are you through in Glasgow?'

'No. I've just been wandering about Edinburgh all day. I'm scared to go home.'

'Why are you scared? What's happened?'

'*Listen, I don't want to talk on the phone. Can we meet up? Lizzie told me she didn't kill Andy Watt and she was passionate about it. But she didn't feel safe. She thought they were going to kill her.*'

'Where are you now, Ben?'

'*I'm at a supermarket round the corner from Fettes Station.*'

'Okay. I know a place you can go that's safe.'

'*Where's that?*'

'Just stay where you are. I'm going to make a phone call and see if a couple of friends of mine can come and pick you up.'

'*Are you sure it's safe?*'

'As safe as you are now.'

THIRTY-ONE

Back then

The patient sat in a grimy chair that looked like it belonged in a landfill. He'd seen shopping carts pulled out of a river in a better state than this. The tin cup he was holding had almost burnt his hand off. 'I have to say, this tea is like pish water.'

'It's all I have, sorry. I can give you a wee kick to it if you like?' The undertaker gave his best creepy smile, and not for the first time the patient felt the hairs on the back of his neck go up. It was why he had brought a Stanley knife along.

'That's fine. I need to keep a clear head.' The patient blew on the tea and took a sip, but his top lip went the same way as his fingers: scalded. He gave up and put the cup down at his feet, making a mental note to boot it over when he got up in case the old bastard recycled the tea bag.

'Remember way back when?' he said, watching the undertaking sitting on the rolling stool.

'I do, yes.'

The room was large and filled with coffins. The place smelled of sawdust and...dust. He saw a pile of white coffin linings in the back corner, waiting to be taken away. Standing up against the back wall were a few coffins with no lining.

'Still up to your old tricks?' the patient said. 'Burn a few bodies without the coffins, resell them and make double your money?'

'Often triple. Times are hard, and those coffins are beauties. Look at them shine.' The undertaker spoke about the boxes as if they were cars sitting in a showroom waiting to be bought by a new owner. Which, in a way, they were. Different items, but the principle was the same: show them the most expensive model, tell them they deserved it – their dearly departed – and then they would sign on the dotted. By the time they came round to this shithole of a funeral home, their eyes would be so full of tears, they wouldn't notice anything amiss. 'I buff them up and we give them a new coat of varnish. I mean, we *do* work on them again. It's not as if we just turn them around and fire them back out.'

'God forbid. And if you miss a scratch, then you can say it got dinged in the hearse?'

'Nobody's ever said a word in all the years we've been doing it.' The undertaker smiled. The presumption of ill-fitting teeth and bad skin was unfounded, but when you were robbing a lot of your customers, you could afford implants, the patient supposed. The man still gave him the creeps.

'But as I was saying, the good old days. I need you to cast your mind back...'

Martin Sutherland was a happy man. The happiness was to prove limited, in fact, but for now he was happy. His one and only son was getting married. This caused swelling pride that one day soon he might be a grandpa, and sadness that his little boy was all grown up and leaving the house.

Of course, if he had had his way, the lad would have been out of the house a long time ago. The boy had an appetite, let his mother do all his laundry and stayed out late more often than not. But he was a bloody good undertaker. He never failed to make it to work no matter how much he'd been on the lash the night before. And he took to the business like the proverbial duck. He worked hard and was a fit heir to take over the business.

So the undertaker overlooked everything else. What did it matter that Neil was staying at home until he got married? He wanted to save for his own home, he had told his mum and dad after he'd announced he'd got engaged.

Sutherland's wife was over the moon, but she had to ask the question: 'Do you *have* to get married, son?' Neil had laughed and said no, that wasn't the case.

Sutherland had shaken his head. 'If they're just getting engaged,' he'd said, 'why would they need to do that? If the lassie was in trouble, they'd be getting married right away.'

Neil had laughed, his fiancée had taken a beamer and they'd all sighed with relief.

That had been two years ago, and now the time for the wedding was upon them, with Sutherland's wife fussing like a mother hen. Sutherland took a back seat. He had offered to drive one of the limos that normally saw service at funerals, and Neil had thought this was a fantastic idea.

Everything was going smoothly. And then one of the groomsmen said they were organising a stag party in a private room in Edinburgh city centre. Sutherland wasn't too keen on that. They lived in Dalkeith and that was bad enough, but the big city was a cesspool at the weekend. But Sutherland didn't want to stand in Neil's way.

'You're coming along too, Dad!' Neil had said.

'Of course I am!' Sutherland replied. 'And the team too.' Sutherland was glad a few of his staff members around his own age were coming along.

The Saturday before the wedding had been warm, it being June. Everything was going great. Sutherland had a good time, downing a few beers with the guys from work, then the stripper had come in and it got raucous, but it was a good time. Sutherland couldn't have been prouder.

Then, outside, it was like stepping into another world. Groups of drunks were going around, singing and shouting. Despite a heavy police presence, one group were out for trouble. They started by asking, 'What the fuck are you lot looking at?'

That might have been the end of it had they ignored the group, but one of Neil's friends told them to fuck off and a fight broke out. Sutherland tried to intervene when he saw his son being punched, but the assailant looked him in the eye as Neil lay on the ground and he grinned as he brought a knife out. Sutherland had never felt such fear. But Neil had reached out from where he was on the ground and grabbed the man's arm, causing the knife to fall. Sutherland smacked it out of the way and his guardian angel kept it going and pushed it into a drain.

But then...the man started shouting and he kicked Neil in the throat and some of the others joined in and they laid in about Neil. Sutherland couldn't help: the man kicked him hard in the guts. Then a police van came screaming into the road and the officers started getting about them.

Neil was pronounced dead at the Royal Infirmary.

The man, Ryan Taylor, was arrested and charged with Neil's murder, but since there was a large group around Neil, no CCTV camera had captured the fatal kick. Taylor denied kicking Neil in the throat, and since it couldn't be determined who'd launched the fatal kick, the charge was dismissed and a verdict of not proven was returned.

Taylor was charged with assault, fined and given community service.

And Martin Sutherland was left to bury his son.

He had never felt such anger against anybody in his life. Then one night, shortly after the funeral, he had taken the hearse and sat outside Taylor's house and started drinking. If the bastard came out, he would run him over.

Then the passenger door opened and a man stepped in. 'Dearie me, you are in the doldrums,' he said.

'What are you doing here?' Sutherland recognised the face.

'Coming to save your skin, old chum. Now, get out of that fucking driving seat before a patrol car passes by. Let me drive.'

And he did.

'You were going to kill that scumbag. He deserves it. I don't blame you, but you've got to be smart about it. You don't want to fuck it up and have him not die and you go to prison for attempted murder. That wouldn't do at all.'

'What am I supposed to do now?' Sutherland said. 'He killed my boy. I witnessed it, I saw him kick my son in the throat. Nobody believed me.' His lip was quivering now.

'First of all, you're not so drunk that you'll forget this conversation. In fact – ' the man held up the bottle – 'not drunk at all. But you would have been and that would have been the end of everything. Now, I'm going to help you get even with that bastard.'

'They'll know I killed him.'

'No, they won't. We'll play them at their own fucking game – and win. You see, when that bastard's gone, you'll have a cast-iron alibi.'

'What's that then?'

'Me. I'm your alibi.'

Sutherland looked at him. 'What do you get out of this?'

'Satisfaction. Seeing the right thing get done. But I have one condition.'

'Which is?'

'You don't question my movements or my ideas. This thing will be planned down to the last detail. And you never ask me again what I'm getting out of it. Deal?' The man held out his hand for Sutherland to shake. Sutherland shook.

'You're not going to like this next bit, but you're going to have to dig deep. You see, timing is everything. This is going to take time. Things have to blow over, until he's not on anyone's mind. Then we'll do it. You have to trust me. Can you do that?'

Sutherland nodded as he mentally pictured Neil

lying on the ground being kicked to death. 'You'd better believe it.'

'And you must never tell anybody.'

'My wife will want to know where I'm going,' Sutherland said.

'Then you will tell her exactly what I tell you to tell her. Understood?'

'Perfectly.'

The patient started the hearse up and drove away. He'd had the foresight to dress like an undertaker, with a white shirt and black tie in case any passing patrol car uniform had a look in. If they got stopped, he'd tell them he was driving for a friend. End of story.

But the drive out to Dalkeith was uneventful and they made it to the funeral home without incident.

'How will you get home?' Sutherland asked. 'How did you even know I would be there tonight?'

'First of all, I'll get a bus back into Edinburgh, and secondly, I could tell by your face when you were in the gallery in court watching that filth walk free that you would be there one night. I constantly drive by there and tonight I saw you.' That wasn't quite true; he'd put a GPS tracker on the hearse and had looked for it moving after hours. But Sutherland didn't need to be bothered by a small detail like that.

'I'll keep in regular touch. Remember, I will not forget about this, but it's going to take time. Time will be on our side if we let it.' And with that, the patient left.

Martin Sutherland went about his business, still feeling the anger grow inside of him, and it was weeks before he heard from the patient again. Just checking in, the patient told him.

And that was how it went. For almost two years. He had thought the patient must have been talking nonsense that night, and Sutherland was about to go out and do something stupid again, but then the patient walked into the funeral home one day, just when Sutherland was closing for the day.

'This is it,' he said simply.

Sutherland's wife's health had been failing. She had never been the same after Neil's death. She had worked in the family business in the office, but after a while she couldn't even do that. She constantly talked about her little boy, and how Ryan Taylor's mother still had her son after he was allowed to walk free even after killing Neil. It ate away at her.

'I think you came in time,' Sutherland said as

they drank a cup of tea in the workshop. The funeral home itself was in the middle of the little town, but the workshop was behind Sutherland's house out in the middle of nowhere.

'Your wife will get a new lease of life when she knows Taylor is missing,' the patient assured him.

'I hope so.'

'Right then, down to business. I'm going to go over a few things, and we have to stick to them. Understand? No deviating from the plan or else we could both end up in prison.'

'I understand.'

'I asked you a long time ago what shoe size you are. I bought you a pair of wellies, two sizes too big. For me too. I bought clothes to be worn on the night and then we'll get changed after we do the deed. The clothes we wore will be put into several coffins, only the ones that are going to get cremated. And metal parts will be taken off first, so it's only cloth that goes in to get burned. The wellies will get cut up and the soles melted with a blowtorch so they can't match the prints even if they did get what's left of them. Everything was bought in England on different day trips, in different stores, using cash. I went at the time of year when it was usual to be wearing a heavy coat and a hat, and I never once looked up at any camera.

The clothes I bought in a charity shop, in the north of Scotland, when I was on a day trip. Using cash. The tools were bought in a big DIY chain store for cash. Again, avoiding cameras, but they won't check the one I went to. Too far away.

'We're going to leave our mobile phones here so they'll ping on the same tower, showing we never left here. We'll communicate by using throwaway phones. When we're done, we'll break them. No photos are to be taken on the burners, and we'll only call or text each other. The phones were bought a long time ago, miles away from here. Lastly, we will not deviate from the plan other than in extreme circumstances. Then you're on your own.'

The patient had a contingency plan in case it all went up shit creek, but that was only for emergencies. He would take steps to cover his own arse.

In the end, he wouldn't have to.

Ryan Taylor didn't think twice about the night he'd kicked the pansy to death. The skinny bastard had actually called out for his mum before Ryan kicked him in the throat. Fucking Nancy-boy. He hadn't thought about the murder in a long time. He had moved on, having done his community service no problem.

Tonight he'd had a good night out. He'd been at his girlfriend's house, had a few drinks and messed about with her, and now he was going home. Unlike his pals, he didn't have to worry about getting up for work in the morning because he didn't work. His parents supported him, but he used the word *support* lightly. They were both a couple of crackheads who didn't know what day it was most of the time.

He was walking across the bridge that spanned the canal when he sensed somebody behind him. He turned round to look, thinking it was some wide boy going to mug him. But it was just some old geezer with a walking stick.

Taylor carried on, walking along the footpath that skirted the Union Canal. It was dark now, not pitch black like in winter but plenty dark. That didn't matter to him, though. It wasn't like somebody would mug him. He'd stab the bastard if they tried anything. He had a quick look round; the old boy was walking behind him, trying to keep up. Maybe he thought if he was near Taylor, nobody would mug him. Not that Taylor would stop anybody from mugging the old bastard. It was what he deserved.

He was almost at the small activity centre where

people kept kayaks and all sorts of sports things in shipping containers. His girlfriend had suggested they rent a bike and cycle along the pathway one day, and he had almost backhanded the stupid bitch. Fucking cycle? He had almost turned down sex that night he was so offended.

'Oh, ya bastard,' Taylor heard the old boy say behind him. He turned round to look. The old bastard had dropped money. *Fucking yes!* He had a few bundles and one of them had scattered over the pathway.

Taylor turned back and walked towards the old boy. 'Need a hand, Grandad?'

'I'm fine, son.' The old man was bent over trying to pick up the money, struggling, leaning on his walking stick.

'Let me help you,' Taylor said, and he started to pick up the money, but instead of handing it over, he put it in his pocket.

'What are you doing?' the old man asked.

'I'm keeping it, ya stupid old bastard. Now give me the fucking rest of it.' Taylor couldn't believe his luck.

Then the man laughed.

'What's so funny?' Taylor asked, his anger rising

now. Maybe he'd take the money and give this old fuck a good kicking into the bargain.

'You think you're so smart, don't you?' the old man said, standing up straight.

Taylor said nothing.

'He does,' another voice said from behind. This man was bulkier, taller and dressed all in black.

'Who the fuck are you?' Taylor said, but then something pinged in his brain. The face was familiar. Where had he seen it before?

'Take a look at the money,' the man said. Taylor took a note out of his pocket and looked at it. A fifty-pound note. Nothing seemed out of the ordinary. Then he saw the words printed on the side: *play money*.

'What the fuck is this?' he snarled, but it was too late. The man with the walking stick had been hiding something in his hand and that thing connected with the back of Taylor's head and the young man fell, unconscious.

'I hope I didn't kill him,' Martin Sutherland said, leaning on the walking stick now, peering down at the prone figure.

The patient smiled. 'No, he's just sleeping. Plenty of time for killing later.'

They picked up the money and put it in their

pockets. This was a crucial part of the plan. There had to be contingencies built into every stage, just in case. In this case, if somebody came along, they would pull their ski masks on and roll Taylor into the canal, then chase whoever it was away. If they didn't run, the stun gun would take care of them, then they would get away in the van.

But nobody came, nobody disturbed them, and they got Taylor into the back of the funeral van, putting him into a coffin.

The patient was sweating now, but he noticed Sutherland wasn't. 'How are you not roasting?' he asked.

'I'm used to this,' Sutherland replied.

They got out into the front. Now they would drive north, to a place that the patient had picked out. It was perfect.

They made the drive in less than two hours. Taylor had been laid in the coffin in the back of the van, bound and gagged, and he stayed unconscious all the way to their destination. Sutherland was worried that the boy was dead, but the patient assured him he was still bleeding and that he had a 'bag of tricks' that would wake the bastard up should it be found that he was faking it.

The two men couldn't carry the young man in the coffin, so they took him out of the wooden box and transferred him into a body bag. Then they carried him to the grave that had been dug earlier. It had been dug over time so that it was deep. It had been well camouflaged.

The trek from the track where the van was parked into the woods was a fair one, but after they carried Taylor they rested, and then they went back for the coffin. Taylor wasn't going anywhere, even if he did wake up in the body bag.

It took an hour for the transfer. They went back and forth, coming back with four petrol cans from the van, which was the hardest part. Then they rested, drinking coffee from a camping coffee pot. They sat round the fire they'd made, the canopy of trees keeping them dry, and the patient listened to Sutherland's stories, and vice versa.

After another hour had passed, Taylor woke up; they could hear his muffled cries from within the bag. The patient got up from the log he'd been sitting on and stretched before pulling the zip down. He was holding a machete he'd brought out from his 'bag of tricks' and he hid it behind his back, prepared to use it.

Taylor panicked and he mumbled a shout which

the patient deciphered as, 'What the fuck are you doing?'

The patient smiled. 'Calm down now. I'm going to take the gag out of your mouth, but if you start shouting, I'll cut your tongue off.' He brought the machete out and Taylor started struggling. This time it was, 'No, no, please!'

Sutherland came over and the two of them lifted Taylor under the armpits and pulled him to his feet. His hands were cable-tied behind his back, and his legs and ankles were also bound. They dragged him over to the campfire and threw him down onto the ground.

The patient removed the gag.

'Who are you? What the fuck are you doing? Do you know who the fuck you're messing with?'

'I told you he was going to be like this,' the patient said, and Sutherland stepped forward and kicked Taylor in the side. The young man groaned and tried to roll into the foetal position but could only manage it so far.

'Bastard,' he said. 'You're a fucking dead man.'

'Really?' the patient said. 'And how would that be? We're here, me and him, and you're tied up, so just how do you think you're going to achieve this?'

'When I get out, I'll find you pair of bastards with my friends and we'll cut you up.'

'You mean you'll kick us to death?' the patient said. He looked over at Sutherland, who seemed incapable of speaking. Maybe his anger was jumbling his thoughts. Maybe he was just enjoying seeing this young scum-bucket lying on the damp ground in pain.

Then he looked down at Taylor and saw the young man's eyes had gone wide. Finally, he had recognised who they were.

'You. You're that old guy...your son...'

'Aye, that's right, ya wee bastard. Not so fucking hard now that your pals aren't around, are you?'

'I'm sorry. I didnae mean it! Please! Let me go! I won't tell anybody.'

Taylor's words almost got to Sutherland, until he pictured Neil lying in his coffin.

'Die, ya bastard,' Sutherland said, and then there was a stillness in the dark air, the only sound the crackle of the burning logs.

The patient nodded and then they grabbed Taylor by the arms again, dragging him away from the fire. Taylor started shouting and moving his bound legs as best he could, but he was no match for the two men. They dragged him towards the grave, dropped him in feet first and let go. Taylor hit the coffin hard and was winded, which stopped him shouting.

'I've waited a long time for this,' Sutherland said, picking up one of the petrol cans. He poured the petrol onto Taylor, who had started up the screaming now. The patient helped Sutherland with the other petrol cans but kept some in the last one and created a trail with it.

'You light it,' he said to Sutherland. The man lit the end of the trail and watched the flames take hold and run for the grave.

Then there was an explosion of fire. The patient thought that maybe they'd put too much in, that the trees would catch fire, but they didn't.

The fire raged on for a while, consuming the coffin and Taylor with it. Eventually, Sutherland fell into a difficult sleep, fuelled by dreams of his son. He woke up to an alarm clock, thinking he had dreamt the whole thing, but the patient was standing over him.

'We need to start working on this before the sun comes up.'

Sutherland nodded and accepted the offer of a hand to get to his feet. He was stiff and sore. He looked over to the grave. There was a dull orange glow in there now, the remnants of the coffin and the body the only source of fuel left.

They each grabbed a shovel and Sutherland looked into the hole and saw the charred remains of Ryan Taylor and the remnants of the coffin and whatever else was down there burning away, little more than embers now.

Then the patient threw in a shovelful of earth and part of the fire went out.

'Cover him,' the patient said. 'You should do this part. Have the satisfaction of burying the man who killed your son.'

'It doesn't bring Neil back.'

'No, but this pond life will never hurt anybody ever again, thanks to you. And he messed with the wrong person when he messed with you. How dare he hurt your boy.'

That was all Sutherland needed to spur him on. He shovelled dirt into the hole until Taylor couldn't be seen anymore.

They finished and were away before sun-up.

It had been years since they'd killed Ryan Taylor and Sutherland had thought that maybe the patient had forgotten. Now, as the man stood smiling at him, he knew that wasn't the case, and a chill went through him.

'And now you're back to call in the favour,' he said.

'Yes, I am. Do this for me and you'll never hear from me again. This will be a very easy job for a man with your skills.'

Sutherland nodded. 'What is it you'd like me to do?'

'Listen carefully and I'll tell you.'

The funeral was a quiet affair. The only person there who was not from the funeral home was the doctor who had pronounced the patient dead. He stood in the rain, getting soaked, his overcoat doing very little to protect him from Edinburgh's inclement weather.

The coffin was brought out of the hearse and carried to the grave, and for a moment Martin Sutherland was reminded of a different kind of funeral back in the forests of Scotland. This time, there was less drama, less fire involved. In fact, the only petrol used was to drive the hearse.

The doctor shook hands with Sutherland, the

first and last time the two ever met. There had been no obituary, not even on the funeral home's website. No announcement to inform people of the patient's passing.

The only other person in the cemetery was a man in a waterproof raincoat and a hat. The fake glasses changed his whole appearance, as did the black goatee.

He watched and waited until the small cortege left, and then walked over to where the gravediggers had covered the grave with a roll of fake grass. He wasn't sure why they didn't fill it in just now, but they were all away. He stood looking down at the grave, at the marker with the name on it.

His name.

He smiled. Now he would be able to finish what somebody else had started.

THIRTY-TWO

Now

It could have been three thugs sitting in his living room, waiting to give him a kicking. After Morgan had been attacked by Lizzie last December in his house, Harry wasn't sure anymore. So he walked in with a smile and a clenched fist, since it could go either way.

'Evening, sir,' Robbie Evans said, and Harry hoped he and the other men couldn't see behind the smile.

'Evening, lads.' Harry looked at Ben Tasker. 'Glad you called, son. You being looked after?'

'I am.'

'We offered him a beer, but there's none here. I think your last tenant must have taken it with him, which wasn't very hospitable of him,' Jimmy Dunbar said.

'I don't think we should be drinking anyway,' Tasker said, standing up and shaking Harry's hand. 'Thanks for listening to me, Harry.'

Harry took his jacket off and hung it on the back of one of the two dining chairs that sat at the little bistro table at the window, overlooking the bowling club.

'Anybody for a coffee?'

'This late?' Dunbar said. 'My bladder's not built like an iron boiler anymore, Harry.'

'You can still put the pints away, though,' Evans said.

'Coffee doesn't get you pished. But why am I explaining this to you?' Dunbar stood up. 'You know what, Harry? I think I will put the kettle on.'

'I don't know if there's any coffee to be honest. I was just being polite.'

'Calvin's coming through to live here tomorrow. His daughter, Carrie, was here stocking up with some staples and she brought some of his clothes through. Hopefully, the lassie is smart and brought coffee.'

Dunbar went through to the kitchen as Tasker stood there awkwardly.

'Bingo!' Dunbar shouted from the kitchen. 'Anybody want one?'

They all answered that they did.

'Robbie! Get your arse through here and start helping,' Dunbar shouted through.

'By helping, he means do it for everybody,' Evans said, leaving the living room. His theory was confirmed when Dunbar came back into the room.

'Right, Ben,' Harry said. 'I need you to explain what you meant when Lizzie said they were going to kill her. Who's *they*?'

'I wish I knew,' Tasker said, taking a seat at the table. There was a folder on it that Harry had seen but ignored. Tasker opened it and took out a pile of drawings, laying them out on the small surface on top of each other.

'What's this?' Harry asked.

'It's Lizzie's drawings. They only let her use crayons, but she enjoyed that.'

Dunbar came across as Harry sat on the other chair, moving it closer to Tasker for a better view of the drawings.

'How often did you go in to see her?' Harry asked.

'I went every couple of weeks. I wanted to go more, but she was concerned for my safety.'

'Don't take this the wrong way, son, but she *was* in a psychiatric hospital. She was obviously delusional.'

'I think the medication they were giving her made her loopy. I mean, I know she was messed up to begin with after being held captive by her step-mother and that other guy, but she wasn't as daft as they were making out.'

Harry was going to correct Tasker regarding the use of non-PC language nowadays, and the term 'being daft' wasn't in the dictionary, but he let it go. They had bigger fish to fry.

'Tell me about the conversations you had with her about her thinking she was going to be killed.'

'She said they were listening to her, which I'm pretty sure is against the rules, but she thought it anyway. Maybe they were hoping to record a confession, even if she was talking to herself, but I don't know if that would be admissible in court.'

'What gave her the idea in the first place?' Dunbar asked.

'She told me she would talk out loud to herself, and one day she was talking about how she loved fried eggs. A couple of days later, an orderly came in with her breakfast tray and said, 'Here's your friend eggs. I hear they're your favourite.' Lizzie thought that had been a mistake, that the orderly slipped up. So she did it again; she said she liked pancakes with strawberry jam, and what do you know? A couple of days later, pancakes and jam. Maybe they thought it would help her open up if they were giving her favourite food, but she just kept talking to herself and drawing her cartoons.'

'What did she say about Andy Watt's death?' Harry asked.

'She said she didn't kill him and she didn't know why somebody would want to frame her. Here, take a look at this.' Tasker looked through the drawings and pulled one out.

Harry looked at it. It was of a van, looking straight at it, face on. There was red coming out from underneath it. And the driver was a figure who was grinning. Standing looking at the van was the figure of a girl.

'I think that's Lizzie,' Tasker said, tapping his finger on the paper. 'Standing in front of the van, watching the killer drive over Andy Watt.' He looked at Harry. 'She told me she had witnessed somebody driving the van. And more to the point, he had seen *her*.'

'And that's why they had to kill her,' Dunbar said.

'Yes.'

There was silence in the room for a moment.

'Coffee,' Evans said, coming into the room with a mug in each hand.

'Cheers,' Dunbar said.' Evans put the mugs down and went off for the other two and was back a minute later.

'Let's assume she was killed,' Dunbar said. 'Who would have done it?'

'Hamish McKinley,' Harry and Tasker said at the same time.

Dunbar looked at Evans before speaking. 'The guy we found in the bin this morning?'

'Same one,' Harry said. 'He was a friend of Lizzie's. They had been outpatients together and were friendly.'

'Lizzie didn't trust many people,' Tasker said. 'She trusted McKinley.'

'Why would he want to kill her?'

'I don't know.'

'We're waiting on the PM being done tomorrow,' Harry said, 'and then toxicology will be done. There were no obvious signs of trauma on her – and I'll have to ask you to keep that to yourself – so the only other alternative is natural causes. Or poisoning.'

'There were some pills found in a baggie in McKinley's pocket,' Dunbar said, 'when we went through them at the scene.'

Harry looked at him and Dunbar gave a very slight shake of his head; he didn't want to say any more in front of Tasker, just in case.

'Turns out that McKinley was going through to see a friend in Glasgow, but the name he gave to his grandmother was false. I don't suppose he was going through to see you, Ben?' Dunbar said.

'Me? God, no. I didn't like him. He's at least ten years older than me. I had nothing in common with him, but he seemed to connect with Lizzie in the hospital. Whoever he was going to see, it wasn't me.'

'What else did Lizzie draw?' Harry asked, changing the subject.

'It started to get weirder. Take a look at this one, for example.' Tasker brought out a picture of a woman in a dress. She had red crosses for eyes as if she was dead, and a dagger with blood on it was lying by her side.

'You spent time going to see Lizzie over the last six months,' Harry said, 'so did she tell you who she thought might kill her?'

'Nobody specific.'

Harry took the drawings and looked through them. They were all variations on a theme, some happy with sun and flowers, others full of despair and danger.

He looked at one of a girl sitting in a room. There was a spider in a web.

'Did you ever feel anything out of the ordinary after you visited Lizzie?' Dunbar asked Tasker. 'Like somebody following you or anything like that?'

'No, nothing like that. I mean, that's not to say it didn't happen. But I wasn't aware of that.'

Harry drank some of his coffee. 'What was Lizzie like up to the point of what happened last Christmas?'

'She was fine,' Tasker said. 'She didn't talk about her dad much, but she adored Maggie. That's what shocks me so much, that Maggie used Lizzie to put you off the scent, like when she used Lizzie's phone and put her prints on a glass. That was sneaky.'

'She was head of forensics in Edinburgh,' Harry said. 'She knew how to manipulate a crime scene.'

'Are you going back through to Glasgow tonight?' Dunbar asked Tasker.

'No. I'm staying with a friend. I'm going to be

staying here in Edinburgh at least until Lizzie's funeral.'

'She had money, didn't she?' Dunbar said. 'I spoke to DSup Stewart after he spoke to you at home last year. You told him she had money from her dad. Money he'd left her in the will.'

Tasker nodded. 'Yes. She had a fair bit.'

'Do you know if she had a will?'

'I'm not sure. I know we lived together, but who thinks you're going to die at our age?' Tasker shrugged. 'She has a box of personal papers in our flat. Maybe there's something in there.'

'Check when you get home.'

'I will.' Tasker looked at his watch. 'I'd better get going.'

'Where does your friend live?' Harry asked.

'Up at Colinton.'

'I'll call you a taxi.'

'Thanks.'

'Do you mind if I take photos of these drawings?'

'You can keep them. I have memories of Lizzie in here,' Tasker replied, tapping the side of his head. 'I don't need the drawings.'

Five minutes later, the cab was waiting downstairs.

'What do you make of him?' Dunbar said once Tasker left.

'I think Lizzie was a sick young woman and her boyfriend got swept up in it all,' Evans said.

'I'm on the fence,' Harry said. 'Lizzie said they wanted to kill her, and then she dies. And a man who was coming in to visit her is murdered.'

'It looks like he was dead a few days before she died,' Dunbar said. 'According to our pathologist.'

Harry nodded. 'These pills he had on him? What do you think they could be?'

'A pal from the drugs squad said probably fentanyl. It's big in America and it's over here. The stuff is deadly. If that was what McKinley gave her, then it could have killed her, and it won't show up until toxicology reports come back.'

'Is McKinley known to your guys through there?'

Dunbar shook his head. 'That's the thing; they've never heard of him. He's a perv with a record and he's on the register, but he's not a known drug dealer. Maybe he was wanting to branch out. But his granny thinks he's harmless.'

'What's your gut telling you?' Harry asked both men.

'It's all wrong,' Evans said. 'McKinley got the drugs from somebody else. He wasn't selling them.

He either bought them or somebody gave them to him.'

'Or the killer planted them on him. There are no prints on the bag. It's been wiped clean,' Evans said.

'Whoever killed him wants us to believe this was about the drugs. But it's about something completely different,' Harry said.

THIRTY-THREE

Bobby 'I've Got a Bad Back' Livingston had just opened his second can of lager when the doorbell rang. He looked at his watch. 'Sake,' he muttered, getting up.

He looked through the peephole. You couldn't be too sure nowadays. There were that many ne'er-do-wells floating about and it wasn't even fucking Halloween yet. That was months away, and Bobby was fucked if he would answer the door then. Wee bastards going about guising, then they'd pull a knife out and rob you. He wasn't going to be fooled like that again.

It was Deek, his pal. He opened the door and ushered him in.

'Keep me standing out there,' Deek complained. He was a tall, skinny bastard with a receding hairline and glasses. How he hadn't been mugged before never ceased to amaze Bobby.

'There's no' a group of Vikings going about raping and pillaging.'

'Wester Hailes is rough,' Deek complained.

'Cheeky bastard,' Bobby admonished. 'Baberton Mains is just an extension of Wester Hailes, divided by the main road.'

'Aye, aye. You ready?'

'It's early. What do you mean, am I ready?'

'You're having a good chow-down I see,' Deek said, nodding to the bag of crisps that was still in Bobby's hand.

'You want one?'

'Aye right. You might have been touching yourself without washing your hands afterwards, contaminating the crisps. I'd be as well scattering a packet in the shitehouse of the pub and eating them off the floor.'

'Och, away and don't talk shite,' Bobby said, heading back to the living room where the plastic clip for the crisps was.

'Your hoover broken down again?' Deek said, nodding in the general direction of the carpet.

Bobby ignored him and found the clip, closing the bag of crisps. He licked his fingers, getting the salt off.

'Manky bastard,' Deek said.

'What? It'll save me wiping my hands on the curtains. It's what I do when I'm round at your hoose and you go to the lav. I just wipe my fingers on the curtains or rub them on your settee.'

'Eh? Minging bastard. I'll never invite you round again. Fucking clart.' He was cut short by Bobby laughing.

'See your face,' Bobby said, laughing.

'Aw, you had me going there.'

Bobby turned away towards the kitchen, hoping Deek didn't see through the lie. The last time he'd been at his friend's house, he'd wiped his fingers on the carpet to dry them after he'd licked them, which wasn't the same as just wiping them on the curtains (which he'd done the previous time). He ran the tap and washed his fingers in the water, just to appease Deek, but truth be told, Bobby wiped his fingers on whatever surface was suitable and available.

'Right, let's get going. The traffic will be light at this time of night.' He looked at his watch: half past midnight.

He and Deek both loved being members of

Tread Well, a group of environmental vigilantes who went around letting the air out of the tyres of big Chelsea tractors, otherwise known as SUVs. Those posh bastards didn't need to have a huge Range Rover in the city to take Farquhar and Focker to their school. They could cycle or take the bus. Truth be told, Bobby couldn't really give a fuck what those people drove their rabid offspring to school in, but he wanted to keep in good stead with Marian. She was the chairwoman of Tread Well, the woman who had started the local action group of like-minded people who went around being what Marian described as 'urban warriors'. Bobby had another word for them and it had nothing to do with urban or warrior.

'They're just a bunch of gormless twats who should go out and get a job so they too can afford a Range Rover,' he had said to Deek one night in the pub.

But Bobby had taken Marian home that first night and had made the mistake of letting her play with Bobby Junior. She couldn't get enough of him after that. He'd yessed and nodded and hmmed and raised his eyebrows at the required times when the melting Arctic Circle was brought up. Marian had thought he was a good listener, but several times during that first spiel – a boring rant by any other name, one that had made him think of taking his belt off and putting one end round his neck and the other round a doorknob – and had asked him if he wanted to join her growing social group. Thinking it had more to do with eating doughnuts than doing anything physical, he had said he would think about it. He didn't want to give her a verbal contract until he learned what he was getting into twice a week.

Then she had said the name Tread Well, and what it entailed, he thought it would be fun. He had dragged Deek into it, telling Marian that he had a friend who would love whatever it was she was offering. Deek had spluttered when he found out, had told Bobby that he was a selfish arsehole who thought of nobody but himself, but when he had reiterated they met in Marian's house once a week and she gave out fairy cakes, Deek had told Bobby that he was the only fairy who would be there, but he'd tag along, 'just for the cakes and tea, mind, nothing more'. Bobby couldn't think of what else Deek was thinking about when he said 'nothing more'. Maybe that they were going to strip down and sit round a bonfire in her back green, playing the guitar and saying 'man' at the end of every sentence.

They had gone to Marian's house, thinking that maybe they were expected to put their car keys in a fish bowl, which would have been awkward on two levels: they'd come with each other and not a member of the opposite sex (although the retired school teacher looked like he wouldn't have minded either way), and neither of them had a car at that moment in time.

But there was no sign of a fishbowl and everybody kept their car keys firmly out of sight, which Bobby felt relieved about. Marian seemed to be the youngest one there and she was in her late forties, while Bobby and Deek had left fifty behind a few years ago. There was Mrs Smith, who had enough make-up on to make her look like she had just escaped from the back room of the local funeral director's. Then there was Pete, who Bobby was convinced just came along for the doughnuts and who looked like he couldn't get enough energy to spray saliva all over the burning candles on a birthday cake, and Clara, who looked old enough to remember the first automobile.

Marian told them that they may be a mature group, but they were still valuable in the fight to protect the planet. Bobby had finished his doughnut, licked his fingers and wiped them on her velour settee before the first hoorah had finished. He'd hoped nobody would notice he'd choried one of the powdered doughnuts during the crowd rallying but Deek had nudged him and made a 'You've got powder round your mouth, ya fat bastard' motion, and there was no chance of wiping his mouth with his hand and running it across Marian's carpet before anybody noticed.

'Give me a napkin,' he had said in a low voice out the side of his mouth to Deek, who had replied with a suggestion of where Bobby could insert it after wiping his mouth with it.

'We all know somebody evil,' Marian had said, and Bobby's heart had skipped a beat at that, convinced he and Deek were going to have to start worshipping the moon.

'Men and women who are literally driving this planet into destruction with their big cars.'

Bobby was lost after that, eyeing up the chocolate ring doughnut before fucking Benny Hill sitting across from him could get it.

'That's why we need to leave them a message: if you keep your car, we'll keep letting the air out of it.'

There was a cheer and everybody started

yakking about what they were going to do and where they would go to do it. Bobby realised that he would have to stay involved in this so he could see Marian again. Deek wasn't so concerned because he was hoping to go out with the barmaid in their local, but Bobby hadn't been in the company of a woman in a long time, so he pretended he wanted to go out and violate somebody's pride and joy.

'And we all want to see photos of your conquest!' Marian had added.

'Fuck this, I'm off,' Deek said.

'Aw, come on, it'll be a laugh,' Bobby told him. 'Shove it up those snobby bastards.'

'This is pish. Touching cars. What are you, ten? Fucking nonsense. You're only after one thing, and as long as she's giving it to you, you'll do anything.'

'It's a worthy cause,' Bobby said, trying out the words for good measure. They even sounded like the ramblings of a madman to his own ears.

'It's bloody vandalism, Bobby, and you know it.'

'Bollocks. You can come along with me and use my phone to take photies.'

Deek had sat looking like he'd just shat himself, but then he relented. 'Aye, okay, just for you. But you owe me. Bloody tyres.'

And that's how they found themselves walking

round at past midnight looking for a big air-poisoning leviathan.

And they found one on Spylaw Bank Road. Bobby thought that all the cars would be parked on driveways behind high walls, but that wasn't the case. There was a Range Rover sitting on the road outside a house. It had a high wall in front of the garden and somebody standing at the top windows would only see them if they were standing on the opposite pavement.

'Perfect,' Bobby said. 'We'll get this fucker here.'

'It still doesn't feel right, us creeping about like a couple of mutants, letting air out of tyres.'

'It just gives them a message. It's not like we're throwing paint over a Van Gogh.'

'Aye, but still,' Deek said, shoving his hands into his pockets like he didn't want to leave fingerprints anywhere. Bobby had no such reservations and put a hand on the front wing to steady himself as he got down on the road, which was rougher than a badger.

'You'd think they'd patch this fucking road,' Bobby complained. 'I nearly bent my bloody ankle there.'

'It's to stop the great unwashed from using it as a rat run. This road would rip your fucking wheel right off. No wonder they drive off-roaders here; they need them to navigate the potholes.'

'Can you imagine me breaking my ankle and you having to wake somebody up to help me? *"Excuse me, but my friend was trying to shag your tyres out there and he hurt himself. Be a good lad and call for an ambulance, will you?"'* Bobby said in a posh voice, laughing.

'Why don't you shout it a bit louder? I don't think the manager in Tanners heard you.' Tanners was their local pub, just round the corner on the main road.

'Och away, man. They're probably all fuckin' ramped up on coke and crack by now. Or they'll be that pished in the morning that they'll never even notice their tyres are flat.'

Bobby unscrewed a tyre valve cover and was starting to press the middle air release when they saw the headlights. In their younger days they would have had time to scarper and stand on the pavement as if they belonged there, two neighbours having a chat before heading inside, but this bastard was giving it the biscuit.

Bobby's knees weren't the best, and his back had long ago given up the dream of being able to transport its owner at a fair clip, so he barely made it to his feet before the SUV hit him at high speed, smashing along the side of the Range Rover, leaving behind death and destruction before screaming off.

Deek started shouting and ran round to his friend. Or what was left of him.

He felt his heart racing, just before he puked at the side of the road.

THIRTY-FOUR

'You're quiet tonight,' Joe Gallagher said to his son.

Ewan finished his can of lager and let out a humongous burp.

'And you wonder why no lassie will stick around, ya manky wee sod,' Joe said, shaking his head and finishing his own can. He felt the air coming up but put an arm over his mouth. 'Jesus, where did you get this lager? I'm sure it should still have a picture of a half-naked woman on it.'

'Don't drink it if it offends you. But it's German; look at the can. Call yourself a connoisseur?'

'Listen, son, as long as it gets the business done, a wee buzz while tasting good. I don't ask a lot in life.'

'I thought you were going to say, a wee buzz and pish the bed.'

'Old age is coming for you too. Mark my words.' Joe shook the can, hinting he wanted another one.

'I'm going to the golf club,' Ewan said.

'Is Bingo coming here first?'

'Aye, he's nearly here. He said the fat bastard Dryve guy is too busy yakking and not getting the boot down.'

'What's Dryve?'

'Like Uber but with serial killers and hoors driving. At least the last two I got were driven by family members from *The Hills Have Eyes*.'

'Just use Uber from now on then.'

'Bingo had a coupon he wanted to use. Save fifty pence or something, but you donate your organs by the side of a country road to a guy with an axe and a carving knife.'

'Is Simon going down with you?' Joe asked.

'Simon? My brother never leaves the house during the day for fear of the sun turning him to ashes. He and his pal play games in his room like they were twelve and he only goes out after midnight. God knows what they get up to.'

'It still irks you that Brian is Cassidy's nephew and she's being pumped by somebody else now.'

'I like Brian,' said Ewan. 'He didn't like his aunt

much. And I couldn't care less who's sharing Cassidy's bed. I've got some irons in the fire.'

'Really? By irons in the fire, you mean you have your favourites at the sauna?'

'That's disgusting. I mean, there's a lassie at work I've been having lunch in the canteen with.'

'Look how that turned out with Cassidy; she works with you, just like that other poor lassie who was murdered, God rest her soul. Maybe you should try the classifieds for a change.' Joe threw his empty can towards the paper bin and it missed. 'Oh, Christ. Pick that up for me when you get up, there's a good lad.'

'For God's sake, lucky that's empty. That could have been a disaster if beer got on the carpet.' Ewan got up from his chair and went over to pick up the can and fired it into the small bin.

'You really need to find yourself a girlfriend,' his father said.

'Look, I wasn't going to say anything, but it isn't just Bingo who's coming tonight. His girlfriend Lexi is coming, and she's bringing her sister along. I pestered Bingo to bring her and now I'm shiting myself.'

'Why? You've been out with a woman before.'

'Chrissie's different; she's Bingo's future sister-in-law.'

'Oh, I see. You have to treat her with respect.'

'I always treat them with respect.'

'Bloody liar.'

'Anyway, Dad, as much as I'd like to stay and be lectured on the ups and downs of a relationship, the car's here.'

'Look at you, peering out the window like you're a curtain twitcher,' Joe said.

'They're here. Do I look okay?'

'You look better than Larry Grayson on a good night.'

'Larry who?'

'Just YouTube it, son.'

'I think you've had enough of that German beer. Don't wait up.'

The driver outside was honking the horn. Ewan walked out of the living room.

'Shut that door!' Joe shouted in his best Larry voice. Ewan came back and shut it.

'Kids nowadays,' Joe said as the front door shut as well.

The car was a small saloon and the driver was so big he spilled over into the passenger side, where Bingo was sitting. He turned round as Ewan got in the back seat with the two women.

'Ewan, this is Chrissie. Chrissie, this is my pal I was telling you about.'

'How you doing?' she said, smiling. She held out her hand for Ewan to shake.

'Terrific,' he said, holding back the question, *What's that fucking smell?* One of them was reeking and he prayed it was the driver.

The drive to Baberton golf club took two minutes and they all piled out. Ewan gave Bingo some money for the fare as the women walked towards the door.

'No tip?' the driver said as Bingo handed over the money.

'Aye, have a fucking shower before you start your shift, fat bastard,' Ewan said under his breath.

'What did you say?'

'Nothing.'

The driver glared at them before leaving.

'Just remember, he knows where you live,' Bingo said.

'He knows where you live too,' Ewan pointed out.

'No, he doesn't. I gave the company the number of the building next door and we were downstairs waiting for him.'

'Aw, shite.'

'Come on, let's get in and have what might turn out to be your last drink.'

Inside, it was quiet, with only the die-hard alkies in having a drink. They got settled in a corner. Chrissie turned out to be very pleasant and Ewan held back on the filth for once.

When the women were away to powder their teeth or something and have a bit of a gossip, Ewan stared at the TV.

'You enjoying yourself, pal?' Bingo asked.

'I am.'

'Maybe you could tell your face.'

Ewan shook his head. 'Remember that copper who came into the lab? Harry McNeil.'

'I remember.'

'He was asking me about Morgan Allan. You remember her?'

'Morgan. Morgan.' Bingo rubbed his chin.

'The woman who worked upstairs from us and was married to David on the golf team who died in a car crash on Christmas Day.'

'Morgan, Morgan,' Bingo said, still rubbing his chin.

'Oh, come on.'

'I'm kidding. I remember her now.'

'He was asking about her,' Ewan said. 'He's been

seeing her. He wanted to know about David. Asking me all sorts of questions.'

'Like what? Where were you the other night when the guy got murdered on the carousel?'

'You're funny. But no, he wanted to know about David having an affair, and what he was like. I told him the truth. And of course, that poured salt in the wound. David was seeing Cassidy on the side, and he had been seeing her on Christmas Day. Then he came along here, looking like he was well pished. You remember that, eh?'

'Oh, yeah! He was here, looking like he was blootered.'

'And everybody thought he was a champ for driving afterwards until he hit the stone bridge and died.'

'Aye, it put the wind up some of the old bastards in here.'

'The thing is,' Ewan said, 'when I was thinking about it later on, I remembered that Morgan too was seeing somebody else. Or at least that was what the rumour mill was saying. She was seeing a lot of this guy who came round to the hospital, but nobody knew for sure if she was sleeping with him or not.'

'Why would they think she wasn't?'

'Because, like Harry McNeil, he was a copper.'

THIRTY-FIVE

'I thought you would have been calling home last night to tell me you were staying over at Morgan's house,' Jessica said.

'I thought so too to be honest,' Harry said. 'But we had a couple of drinks and a bite to eat, and then she went home on her own.'

Jessica sat down at the dining table, holding Grace. 'Harry, it's not my place to criticise, but after six months of going out with somebody, it's natural that they would have you back to their house. I mean, Morgan's stayed over here before.'

'I know. She says it's because of the bad memories in her house. She's planning on selling up and moving into a smaller place.'

'That would be the answer, but to think she's a

psychiatrist and can't deal with something that happened over ten years ago is a bit ridiculous.'

'I know. I mean, it's coming up for a year since Alex died and I miss her every day.'

'But it didn't stop you bringing Morgan home. Not because you didn't love Alex or it's a slight on her memory, but because it's life, Harry. Life moves on. Alex would understand that.'

'It was strange being in the flat with Jimmy and Robbie and that other guy last night,' Harry said. 'It brought back some memories, let me tell you.'

'And you're going there again this morning to meet Calvin.'

'Aye. To be honest I should just sell it, but something's holding me back.'

'There's no need to sell it. Think of it as an investment for Grace.'

'Yeah, I'll keep it for her and I'll sign it over to her when she's eighteen.'

They were listening to the radio and the news came on. It led with the hit-and-run death of a man near Juniper Green. *'He is believed to be a member of the group Tread Well, who go around letting the air out of the tyres of big SUVs. The police are not ruling out foul play, but so far investigations are leading them to believe that the victim, fifty-four-year-old*

Robert Tompkins, was hit by a drunk driver. The car has not been identified. Anyone with information is urged to call the police.'

'Holy moly,' Jessica said. 'I've heard of those people. They're a pain in the arse. You'd better watch your SUV or they'll be letting your air out.'

'It's not worth killing somebody over.'

'Maybe it wasn't an irate car owner, just somebody giving it yahoo who didn't see him.'

Harry finished his coffee and gave Grace a kiss before pulling on his jacket and leaving the house, still with an uneasy feeling. Was his relationship with Morgan going to go much further? He honestly didn't know. He had feelings for her, but she needed to relax a bit more sometimes.

He drove down to Comely Bank, joining the rank and file going to their offices, clogging Edinburgh's streets. He thought of his interview with Dale Wynn's ex-wife and how she'd said Wynn had been passionate about green issues in Edinburgh and that the council were upside down, cutting off rat-runs and actually adding to the pollution in the city centre. He had to agree. He would go electric one day, but for now petrol was the way. He saw Wynn's point of view and wished the people high up would start improving the electrical grid, but he knew as soon as all the cars relied on electricity, the greedy bastards would shove the price up.

He could start to feel his blood boiling, so he put on an '80s music station. Music from back in the day when electric cars weren't even thought of.

He parked opposite the flat and looked in his driver's mirror and saw a big man get out of a nondescript Ford Mondeo further back.

Calvin Stewart. The bastard was early.

'Harry, son, thanks again,' Stewart said after opening Harry's door. He'd grabbed a bag from his car, a large holdall.

'No problem, sir.'

'Pish. It's Calvin when we're not on duty.'

Harry locked the Jaguar.

'Nice car,' Stewart said. 'Drug dealing must pay well these days,' he added with a smile, and one of Harry's older neighbours looked over and then scuttled away, hauling her shopping trolley behind her.

'You'll be the one living here. They'll think you're the kingpin.'

'Shite, aye, I didn't think that last smartarse remark through.'

They walked across the road to the stair entrance and walked up to the top floor.

'I was thinking of getting my groceries delivered,'

Stewart said. 'Fuck this for a game of soldiers, booting it up here with bags, especially when I've got cans of peeve in them.'

They got to the top landing and Harry's old neighbour and friend Myra came out on her way to work.

'Hi, Harry!' she said, stepping in for a hug. 'It's been a while. How are you doing?'

'I'm doing fine, thanks. Myra, this is my new tenant, Detective Superintendent Calvin Stewart.'

'Nice to meet you.'

'Likewise,' Stewart said.

'Grace doing well?' she asked Harry.

'Grace is blooming.'

'Terrif. Listen, I have to go or I'll miss the bus, but good seeing you again. I'll see you around, Calvin.'

'Will do.'

Harry fished the keys out as Myra shot down the stairs.

Inside, the place smelled fresh, which he had hoped for, as he'd told the last tenant there was no smoking and that he was a copper and he'd better not come in and find any funny scents.

'Right, which way to the master bedroom suite?' Stewart said.

'Hardly a suite.'

'No en-suite bathroom?'

'No maid service either.'

'Dearie me, the facilities in Edinburgh are woefully lacking.'

'To the right,' Harry said. 'Kitchen straight ahead, bathroom on the left, bedrooms on the right, second one is the master.'

'Magic.' Stewart opened the door to the master bedroom and went in, putting his bag on the floor.

'Have an en suite in Glasgow, did you?' Harry asked.

'Behave yourself. It was a lot smaller than this place. This will do me great, Harry, son. I'll fit right in here, so I will.'

'You can have anybody staying over that you want. It's your place now.'

'But?'

'But Myra next door is a bit vulnerable. She broke up with her boyfriend a couple of months ago. She has a cat called Sylvester –'

'Let me stop you there, pal; I have no interest in the neighbour. If I find my own girlfriend, it won't be her next door. She seems nice, but what if we broke up? How fucking awkward would that be? Go out the door for your morning paper and get a fucking pan smacked over your melon? I don't think so. I'll keep an eye out for her, though. Show me the living room before we leave for work. I want to make sure the TV's working.'

They went through and Stewart beamed a smile. 'Nice. A big screen.'

'The only thing you have to do is register for utilities –' Harry started to say, but then he stopped and looked at the photo on the wall unit. The glass was broken in the frame, and he silently cursed his last tenant for being clumsy. It was a photo of Alex and himself he'd left in the flat. Harry had put away in the drawer, but the tenant must have put it back before he left.

At first, Harry thought it had been accidentally broken, but when he looked closer, he saw that somebody had drawn on Alex's face. On the eyes somebody had drawn two little Xs.

Why would his last tenant have vandalised it?

Stewart slapped him on the shoulder. 'Right, pal, let's get across the road and we can get down to business. These murders aren't going to solve themselves.'

Harry quickly put the photo in one of the drawers in the unit.

'Is that broken?' Stewart asked.

'Aye. My last tenant must have dropped it.'

'Clumsy bastard.'

They walked out and Harry gave Stewart the keys, but he wasn't paying attention to Stewart now.

If the last tenant had broken the photo frame, why had he put it back? To make it look like it wasn't broken.

No. It wasn't the tenant. The photo hadn't had the Xs on it before and he knew the man wouldn't have done that.

Somebody else had.

'That was nice of you, to send a lassie over to help my Carrie yesterday,' Stewart said.

Harry put a hand on his boss's arm before he could walk down the stairs. 'Lassie?'

'Aye. Stacey Mitchell, she said her name was. Does she clean the house by any chance?'

Harry thought about it for a second. 'No, I don't know who she is or why she was in the flat. Maybe she's a new girlfriend of my last tenant.'

'Oh, right. I thought she might be interested in washing my skids. Never mind.'

They walked down and went to their cars, Harry desperately wanting to know who Stacey Mitchell was.

THIRTY-SIX

Unlike Calvin Stewart, Finbar O'Toole had travelled through to Edinburgh the evening before so his wife could help him get settled into the serviced apartment in Fountainbridge.

'You're not going to be too lonely without me, I hope,' she'd said.

'Of course I am.'

'I was joking.' Irene had stepped forward and gave her husband a hug.

'I know you were.'

'Liar.' She stepped back from him. 'You're got your work cut out, working with that female who lost her boyfriend.'

'Kate's hurting, but she's a professional. We talked at great length when I got the interview and we hit it off. She's English; I can tell she's trying hard to culture her accent, but now and again the cockney slips out.'

'Good,' Irene said. 'And I'll come through every weekend and we can look at houses.'

'I can't wait. We'll get a nice place.'

'Oh, God, Fin, we've been through so much.'

'I know we have. I thought I could make it as an investigator, but it's not for me. God knows how big Muckle McInsh does it.'

'He's an ex-detective. He's used to the work.'

'And Vern and Shug.'

'They make a great team.'

'Right,' Finbar had said, 'let me get unpacked and we'll go and have dinner.'

Which they did. And it had been great, and he'd walked Irene down to Haymarket Station, five minutes away. That had been a consideration when he took this place, walking distance from the station up to Grove Street. He loved the public transport in Edinburgh now that they had the trams. But he'd have to drive to work, which was no big deal.

He wondered how Calvin was getting on with his first day in Edinburgh. This was a bit of a culture shock for both of them, but he would meet up regularly with the big guy for a few beers. He'd hated the man when he first met him through in Glasgow and he was a pathologist there, but they had become firm friends.

Finbar looked at his watch. Time to go.

It had been years since he had driven here, and it was almost like the city centre had been picked up and a new one dropped in its place. After what seemed like a session on the dodgem cars, he finally made it to the mortuary in the Cowgate and parked next to one of the dour vans. It was painted a dull grey, but then again, he wouldn't have expected a mortuary van to be painted like an ice cream van.

It was a warm morning, and he carried his jacket over his arm as he walked up to the freight entrance and rang the bell.

The side door opened and a young woman answered. She smiled at him and spoke with a Polish accent. 'You must be the new doctor?'

'How do you know I'm not a serial killer about to come in and slaughter you all?'

'You rang the buzzer three times, just like Professor Chester told you to do. It's code for people who know to do that. Come in.'

Finbar stepped over the threshold feeling like an arse for making that glib comment. He smiled as the woman shut the door. 'Please excuse my sense of humour,' he said, hoping the darker interior masked his beamer. 'Your assumption was correct: I'm Dr Finbar O'Toole.'

'I'm Sticks. I'm a drummer in a band when I'm not carting dead people around.'

'Pleased to meet you, Sticks.'

'And here we have Gus Weaver, our retired assistant, but he came back part time.'

'That's quite a mouthful,' Finbar said, shaking the older man's hand.

'Call me Gus. Professor Chester will be in a little bit later today and he sends his apologies. Dr Kate Murphy is waiting for you.'

'We met already at my interview.'

'Oh, yes, Kate said you came from Glasgow,' Sticks said as the three of them walked across the loading area.

'That's right. I had a break for a while,' Fin replied, leaving it at that. He had transferred from Inverness to Glasgow to investigate his niece's death, had helped prove it was really murder and had then found he couldn't work in the mortuary anymore. Now he was ready to grab hold of the reins again.

Kate Murphy was in her office waiting for him. 'Hello again,' she said, shaking his hand. Fin knew all about Andy Watt and no more needed to be said on the matter.

'Would you like a coffee?' Gus Weaver asked.

'No, thanks.' Fin didn't add, *'It'll make me piss like a horse.'*

'Good to see you again, Fin,' Kate said. 'Not a lot of doctors like to go by their first name, but we don't stand on ceremony here. The clients don't mind.'

He laughed at her gallows humour.

'You were updated on your first task today?' Kate asked.

'Yes. The young woman from the psychiatric hospital.' Lizzie Armstrong, the woman who had been sent to the hospital for allegedly killing Kate's boyfriend.

'Obviously, I can't be involved in that, but toxicology has already been sent away.'

'I understand. I'm looking forward to working with you, Dr Murphy.'

She raised her eyebrows at him.

'Kate,' he added. She smiled at him, and Fin knew he was going to be a lot happier here in Edinburgh than he had been in Glasgow.

THIRTY-SEVEN

'Well, well, Charlie Skellett, skulking about in a dark corner. I hope you've got your fucking troosers on,' Stewart said, walking into the incident room. Skellett's desk was indeed in the corner and he'd somehow managed to fiddle with the overhead fluorescents and move some filing cabinets round so he was sheltered from the rest of the room.

'Of course I have. Good to see you again, sir.'

'How's that leg of yours? Although I hate myself for asking.'

'It's getting better, but not as fast as I'd like. In fact, if you can take a look, you'll see for yourself.'

'Fucking watch me. It's like being in a Hammer horror film with you, Charlie. You get lured round the back of his cabinets and he's whipping it oot like a fucking madman.'

'I got myself one of those wee back scratchers,' Skellett said, 'you know, like a telescoping claw. Just like we used to use in the back of the van when we were on surveillance jobs together, remember?'

'I remember fuck all. You're confusing me with another Calvin Stewart, and if that shitey claw thing comes near me, I'll ram it up your arse. Now, who's getting the kettle on? Elvis? Good man. Make my coffee strong and don't let Charlie boy there go anywhere near it before he boils his hands.'

'Sir.' Elvis got up from behind his desk as Stewart looked around the room. 'Who else have we got in today? Lillian and...where's Frank Miller?'

'He's away with Julie Stott looking over videos of Lizzie talking to them back when she was arrested,' Skellett said from behind.

'What are you doing out of your cave? People will start to think you're fucking normal if they see you in daylight.'

One of the phones rang as Skellett walked over towards the kettle.

'Red alert, Charlie's wee claw is on the move. Don't be touching any of the coffee paraphernalia with that thing.'

'Bastard brace still itches. You know, my wife sleeps on a recliner in the living room because she says I toss and turn all night. When my brace is off, that's when the pain gets worse, and of course my leg is minging with sweat. Sir Hugo doesn't mind me in bed, though.'

'You and your dug. Don't be saying that too loud outside.'

Elvis made the coffees and Lillian held up the phone. 'For you, sir,' she said to Harry. He took it and listened before hanging up.

'Everybody listen up. Have we all heard about the hit and run last night?'

They all agreed that they had.

'That was a DS from Wester Hailes. They ran the victim's name through the system in case he was a target for somebody, and it turns out he has form. Bobby Livingston. He was arrested eight years ago on drugs charges, but he denied they were his, and to cut a long story short, he walked free.'

'Why did the DS call you, Harry?' Stewart asked.

'Because I was the arresting officer.'

Just then the door to the incident room opened and Dunbar and Evans walked in.

'Morning, gentlemen,' Stewart said, genuinely pleased to see them.

'Morning, sir,' they both said.

'Right, let's get the coffee going and you can all catch me up on what's been going on. Where's my office?'

'The one next to mine,' Harry said.

'Magic. Evans, go and make sure everything's there and that they haven't swapped in some piece of shite chair for a good one.'

Evans went into the office and came back out a second later. 'Seems fine to me, sir.'

'That means it's fucked, then.' Stewart took the mug of coffee from Elvis and sat down at a spare desk. 'Right, get me up to speed.'

Lillian walked up to their whiteboard and pointed to the photo of Dale Wynn. 'He was out at the fairground with his girlfriend, and they were about to go home when he got a phone call. He said he wouldn't be long, told her to go ahead, and she left to get the fish suppers, and he was killed in the Meadows, on the carousel. We don't know who called yet, as we don't have his phone and it's switched off. The mobile company has been issued a warrant so we can get his records.'

'I don't think anybody would be that stupid to

use their own phone to call him just before they murdered him,' Skellett said.

'You know, Charlie, that's remarkably lucid of you,' Stewart replied.

'Then we have the victim from Glasgow. If you would like to tell us about that man, sir?' Lillian looked at Dunbar.

'Go on, Robbie, you're up,' Dunbar said.

Evans walked forward to stand next to Lillian and she smiled at him.

'Better keep an eye on that pair,' Stewart whispered to Dunbar. 'I think she has an eye for him.'

'Right, Hamish McKinley,' said Evans. 'He was found in an old industrial estate, dressed in a rain jacket and dress trousers, shirt and tie, like he was on his way to meet somebody. He had a bag of pills in his pocket that we think might be fentanyl. They're away being analysed and we should hear today. If it is fentanyl, then we know it can kill easily. He was a friend of Lizzie Armstrong's. We don't know why he was through in Glasgow and neither does his granny, who he lived with. McKinley too was questioned by DCI McNeil years ago.'

'I don't remember him. Was he arrested for anything?' Harry asked.

'No, sir, but his friend was questioned when a

wee boy was taken from the promenade down at Cramond. Tommy McArthur. Hamish gave him an alibi. Cast iron. The granny backed him up, said they were both in the house at the time of murder, despite McArthur inadvertently having his photo taken down on the promenade. McArthur said Hamish was just further along and they were supposed to meet two girls, but the girls stood them up, so they went home. They gave us the girls' names, but they were fake, and they said the girls must have made up the names. They had met them in a pub, they said, and they wanted to meet somewhere public. We had to let them go because there was absolutely no evidence of McArthur or Hamish having any connection with the wee boy, Cormack.'

'Christ, now I remember,' Harry said. 'Creepy bastard he was.'

'McArthur was found deid later on, wasn't he?' Skellett said.

'He was, aye. Suicide, the ruling was. He hung himself in the woods in Cammo,' Harry said.

'Did it look anything other than a suicide?' Stewart asked.

Harry shook his head. 'No. He chose a tree to jump off and did it. The pathologist noted that there were bits of rope under his fingernails, so it seems he regretted jumping and tried to get the rope off, but it had tightened too much. The pathologist said this happens a lot: they're suicidal, but right at the moment of go, they change their mind and try to reverse their decision, but it's too late.'

'I watched a documentary on the Golden Gate Bridge jumpers,' Dunbar said, 'and believe it or not, some of them survived. A lot of them said they regretted doing it as they launched themselves off and they thought it was too late. But they lived to tell the tale.'

'And McArthur's friend Hamish didn't help him on his way?' Stewart asked.

'No,' Harry replied, 'he had an airtight alibi.'

THIRTY-EIGHT

Back then

Christ, did it always rain in Edinburgh, or just days when there was a funeral, the doctor thought as they got out of the car into the downpour. The rain hit the trees like fat on a frying pan and the air smelled thick with wet vegetation.

Mary was a Gorgie lass through and through and she'd wanted to be buried beside her family. That was her wish and the doctor wanted to carry out that wish, even though he thought he was carrying it out thirty years too early. At forty, her life had come to an abrupt end with the aid of a bottle of pills.

She wanted to be with her little boy, the note had

said. She told him she was sorry, but he would be able to go on without her, and her little boy was lying in the ground all alone, waiting for Mummy to come to him to keep him safe.

The doctor had come home to find her in a bath that had been hot when she got in it but was now lukewarm. Mary's face told him all he needed to know, that no amount of help would save her, but the screaming in his head made him call for an ambulance. Just in case.

They had come, they had tried, but another doctor arrived and pronounced her dead. The police had arrived and done what they had to do, but later on, after her time of death was confirmed, the doctor's alibi had been confirmed. Just to rule him out, they said. He didn't have the fight in him to argue.

Now they were here, Mary being laid to rest near her family and their little boy. The doctor was the only one left. Mary had no siblings, her parents were both dead and somewhere else in this place lay a few aunts and uncles.

He barely held it together. Nobody was there for him. He had a sister, but they were estranged. Out of duty he'd called her, and she had asked him one simple question fuelled by a bottle of booze: *'What do you want me to do about it?'* He had hung up, disconnecting the call and disconnecting her from his life.

On the day of the funeral, colleagues had come from the hospital, nobody he would really call a friend, but they shook his hand and said the required words of comfort, but there was one man who approached and stood nearby: the patient. Of course, he wasn't the patient then, but that was how the doctor would come to think of him. Not *a* patient, but *the* patient.

He was wearing a raincoat and held a black umbrella over his head, just like the others. Nobody would remember him. He was just another mourner who would go home that night and thank God it hadn't been them burying a loved one.

The minister gave his eulogy, and the funeral broke up. There was no wake afterwards, no celebration of a life gone too soon. How could they drink and laugh when the woman they had just put in the ground beside her son had taken her own life?

So, the doctor went round the corner to the Athletic Arms, known as The Gravediggers by the locals, and ordered himself a pint. He was hanging his coat up, preparing to drown his sorrows, when the patient walked in. The man ordered himself a pint and approached the doctor as if he was merely an acquaintance, which he was, more or less.

'Sorry again about your wife,' the patient said, and they made their way to a table in a corner. The lunchtime drinkers were gone, and the pub was having a breather before the after-work onslaught.

'It's funny how life can take you down a road that you never expected to go,' the doctor said, and he gripped his glass hard, like he was trying to break it into a million pieces.

The patient put his hand on the doctor's arm until he relaxed.

'It's just so unfair,' the doctor said, staring into his pint. 'Right now I should have been at work while my wife was at her work and our little boy in school. Now they're both in the ground and I'm sitting here in the pub, utterly alone. I have no friends, not any best friends anyway, no family, no nothing.'

'You have me. I'm your friend.'

The doctor nodded and the patient thought he was going to argue for a moment, but he just took a deep breath and let it out slowly.

'It's time,' the patient said.

'For what?'

'It's time you and I went fly fishing.'

'Fly...' But the doctor stopped and looked at the

patient. He had asked him a long time ago, *'How will I know when it's time?'* And they had agreed on the words 'fly fishing'.

'It is?'

The patient nodded. 'It is.'

'When?' The doctor kept his voice down now.

'Well, this is Friday, so how about tomorrow?'

For the first time in a long time, the doctor smiled. 'That sounds good.'

It was easy getting Tommy McArthur into the car. They just scooped him up from outside the Wester Hailes hotel as he was walking home in the dark. The rain helped. They stopped the car and the doctor wound the window down, keeping the interior lights off, and shouted, 'Hey, Tommy! How are you doing? Need a lift?'

And Tommy, being drunk, got in and they drove further down the road and the doctor stopped his car. 'There's a pal of mine. You don't mind if I stop and give him a lift, do you?'

He stopped whether Tommy minded or not, but he just lolled around in the front seat as the back door opened and the friend got in.

The doctor took off, and Tommy was trying to tell the doctor that he had driven past his street when the belt came over his head from the back. He tried to prise it off but failed, and then darkness took him.

They drove round to the Sighthill industrial estate, where the doctor checked for vital signs.

'That would have been a big disappointment if you'd actually killed him in my car.'

'That would have been a big clean-up job, Doc, I'm not going to lie. Fortunately, I've done this before.'

The doctor knew better than to ask any questions.

They got Tommy out of the front seat and into the back, where they buckled him in and put an empty bottle on the seat beside him. If they got pulled over, then they were on a boy's night out and one of them had got blootered.

They drove down the bypass to Turnhouse Road at the Gogar Roundabout and along Turnhouse, connecting with Cammo Road further up, and then drove quietly round the tight little road until they got to the Cammo Estate car park. It was empty in the dark with the rain lashing down.

The patient dragged Tommy out the back of the

car, and he moaned and groaned but didn't wake up. That was okay, he'd wake up in a minute.

The doctor grabbed the rope from the boot of the car after putting gloves on. The patient had already had his on when he got in the car and hadn't taken them off since.

They carried Tommy along a footpath and found the tree that the patient had scoped out on a previous visit. One that would be easy to climb for Tommy and sturdy enough to take his weight when he jumped off.

The patient brought out the smelling salts and Tommy fought them for a moment, but then the shock of the ammonia kicked in and he was awake. By that time the rope had been thrown over the tree and the patient stood behind Tommy, holding his arms.

'Remember me, you fuck?' the doctor said to him in the dark.

'Who...are you?' Tommy asked.

'You were there the day my little boy went missing. You had an alibi, but there was nobody else in the frame. You took him, didn't you?'

'No...no, of course not.'

Tommy was shaking now. The patient could feel it as he held him close.

The doctor grabbed Tommy by the hair, yanking his head back. 'Lying bastard,' he said through gritted teeth.

'I'm not. I didn't touch him. Please!' Tommy's voice was getting louder, so the patient put the rope over his head and pulled tight. The doctor grabbed the other end and started hauling Tommy off his feet. Tommy grabbed at the rope, kicking his legs.

Before his throat constricted entirely, Tommy looked at the doctor and in a croaked voice spoke to him.

'The little bastard died screaming and crying for his mummy!'

The doctor felt a jolt go through him and he let go of the rope and Tommy fell back to the ground. The doctor was on his knees near Tommy now and the man was smiling at him. They locked eyes for a moment.

'Screaming,' Tommy said, and then suddenly he was on his feet and the doctor thought he was going to be attacked and he would have loved that, would have loved to rip Tommy apart, but then Tommy was going higher and higher until his feet were well off the ground. This time there was no reaching for the rope.

The patient came over to the doctor and helped

him to his feet, and the doctor realised in that moment that he wouldn't have been able to fight off a gust of wind, far less Tommy had the man really been coming for him. He was emotionally and physically drained.

They got in the car, the patient driving this time.

The doctor had known what to expect as they'd talked about it over and over, but for now he sat and cried in the passenger seat as the patient drove through the darkness.

Tommy's body was found the next day. Questions were asked and suspicions were raised, but Tommy's friend confirmed that Tommy hadn't been feeling himself lately. He tried to make the junior detective feel bad, make him think that the police had driven Tommy to suicide, but all that did was confirm what they had been thinking all along: that Tommy had hanged himself in the same woods where he had killed the little boy.

The doctor was informed but not questioned. There was nothing to question after all.

If anybody else had any suspicions after that, they didn't voice them. Tommy McArthur was cremated with no fanfare except for a story in the red-tops, and his ashes were scattered by the funeral director.

And that was it, done and dusted. But before they parted ways, the patient met with the doctor one more time in the pub. They talked about fishing and cars and the state of the country. And one more thing.

The patient told the doctor he would be back one day when he needed a favour. The doctor nodded, and they shook on it. And the doctor didn't see the patient again until years later, when he came into his office to cash in his chips.

THIRTY-NINE

Now

'She's barry, isn't she?' Bingo said, bouncing up and down on his heels. Ewan Gallagher was staring off into space. 'Are you listening?'

'No.'

'I said, she's a cracker, isn't she? Chrissie, I mean.' Bingo took his red glasses off and breathed on each lens, taking a cloth to them.

'Aye, aye, she's barry.'

'Dial your enthusiasm down a wee bit, why don't you?'

'I've got a lot on my mind this morning, Bingo.'

They were standing at Ewan's lab bench.

'Chrissie's already called Lexi and said she had a good time and when are we doing it again? How about this weekend?'

'This weekend? I'm not sure. I mean she's a nice lassie –'

'You're the one who wanted this.'

Ewan smiled. 'Keep your fucking wig on. I was going to say, doesn't she want just me and her to go out? Or does she think I keep a hammer in my car?'

'Oh, right. No, she just had a good laugh, that's all. She was in a relationship and it turned sour. He was a chimney sweep.'

'So she jacked in the sweep and went out with Sooty instead?'

'That's not even funny. I mean, chimney sweep? Who does that anymore? What do you say to the careers counsellor at school, I want to stick a brush up my lum?'

'Why would you want to stick a brush up your bum?' Ewan said just as Caroline walked past, and she gave Bingo a funny look.

'Ignorant bastard. You really aren't listening to me, are you?'

'I am, but my mind is on something else.'

'You're not thinking about Harry McNeil again,

are you? Because, let me tell you, mate, you're giving him too much head space.'

'It's just the conversation we had the other day. About Morgan Allan's husband.' Ewan looked at his friend. 'I liked David a lot. I know he was a player, but he was a good guy. They were both at it, cheating on each other, like they had an open marriage. For people to think that David was the cheater and Morgan was squeaky clean, that's just not right.'

'Don't worry about it. It was a long time ago.'

'Aye, but it's strange that McNeil would come here wanting to know about David, that's all.'

'Just forget about it,' Bingo said.

But Ewan couldn't forget about it.

FORTY

DS Julie Stott came into the room with two coffees on a cardboard carrier and set them on the table.

'Your eyes bugging out of your head yet?' she said, sitting down.

'Cheers,' Frank Miller said, taking one of the coffees from the holder. 'Not yet, but they feel like they're on fire I've been staring so hard.' He took a sip of the hot liquid. 'How about you?'

'My backside would have been a lot number if we hadn't brought these office chairs in.' She took her own coffee and sipped it. She and Miller had been in since six a.m. and she was flagging a bit now after four hours.

They'd already watched the police interview tapes with Lizzie, but there was nothing interesting on them. Now they were looking at the hospital ones, given to Miller once he had a warrant issued for their release. They had videos of therapy sessions from before and after Lizzie's arrest for attacking Morgan Allan in Harry McNeil's house with a knife. The video they were watching now was from a session before that incident. Miller wanted to see if Lizzie had spoken about killing herself then. None of the later videos had her talking about suicide. Working with Morgan had helped Lizzie get through her fear, Miller thought.

Miller un-paused the video and it started to play again. Dr Thomas Burke, psychiatrist, entered the room. Burke did a strange thing before Lizzie came in: he stood on a chair and fiddled with the camera before stepping back down. Miller couldn't see why: the sound and picture were just the same as before he'd touched the camera. Burke sat down opposite the young girl. The room was made out like a living room, making it look more personal and safe, rather than the clinical environment of an interview room.

'Lizzie, please feel relaxed in here with me. I'm here to help you. Do you want to talk about your mother keeping you in the church?'

Lizzie sat in a comfy chair with her knees pulled up to her chest, not saying anything for a moment.

'She's not my mum,' she said after a short while. 'She never really treated me like her own flesh and blood.' Lizzie snapped her head towards Burke. 'Maybe that's why she found it easy to lock me in the basement of that place. Then drag me upstairs to that dingy little flay at the top of the church. I thought they were going to kill me.'

'You were scared, Lizzie. We talked about that already, remember? It's fine to feel that way, but you're not going to let it define you.'

Lizzie said nothing.

'Was it because you were scared that you went to Harry's house?' Burke asked gently.

Lizzie looked him in the eyes. 'No.'

'Were you scared when you went to Andy Watt's house?'

'No.'

Burke sat back in the chair as if Lizzie would reach over and smack him one, and he kept a tight grip on the pencil, maybe thinking where the best place to stab her would be. Morgan had told Harry that she'd had a few patients attack her; that was why she'd honed her self-defence skills.

'You were at Andy Watt's house, though, yes?' Burke said.

'Yes, I was. I watched as the man ran him over in the van.'

'The man who haunts your dreams?'

'No. That's somebody else. He doesn't have a face, the man I dream about. The man in the van is different.' Lizzie looked up at the camera.

'This man, did you see him on the day Andy died?'

Lizzie nodded and closed her eyes for a second before looking back at Burke. 'Yes. He was driving the van.'

'I thought you were driving the van, Lizzie.'

Then she did something that surprised Miller: she glowered at Burke. 'I told you I never drove the van.'

There was an intensity about her words and features. A determination, Miller thought. He'd sat across from a lot of people who had been accused of something, and the innocent ones were always passionate about their answers, shouting, trying to convince him that they were innocent because they saw themselves being put away for something they didn't do.

He saw that passion in Lizzie in that moment.

'How about going to Harry McNeil's house? Why did you go there?'

Lizzie looked up at the camera again and shrugged. 'Because she told me to.'

'Who did? Your mother?'

Lizzie shook her head.

'*She* did.'

Burke sat up straighter. 'Your mother told you to do it, Lizzie.' It sounded to Miller like it was a statement more than a question.

Lizzie shook her head and buried her face in her knees and refused to talk anymore. Burke waited for an orderly to take Lizzie out before standing on the chair again and touching the camera. He got down and quickly left the room.

Miller got up and switched the TV off and ejected the tape and put it back in its box.

'I think I'd like to go and talk to Dr Burke. I think he's retired, but we can get his address from the hospital. Or maybe Harry could get it from Morgan.'

They went through to the incident room, where Calvin Stewart was.

'Frank, son, glad you could join us.'

Miller couldn't figure out if Stewart was being facetious or not. 'Hello, sir,' he said. 'Welcome aboard.'

'We're just going over this case.'

'I'd like to have a word with Harry,' Miller said,

'if you don't mind. I'd like to follow up on something that might be nothing.'

'That's fine.'

'I'll take Julie Stott with me since she's been watching the videos with me.'

Stewart turned round. 'I didn't see you there, hen,' he said to Julie. 'Has this laddie got you going all over the place?'

'We've been watching taped video interviews with Lizzie Armstrong.'

'Tapes? When were they filmed, the '80s?'

'They keep them on tape because of privacy issues,' Julie explained. 'The CCTV cameras are digital, but the interviews are on tape for now. That way it makes it harder for somebody to get hold of the interviews and do something nefarious with them.'

'Ah, right. Do what you've got to do.'

Miller asked Harry to call Morgan. Which he did.

FORTY-ONE

The patient parked the car in the little library car park next to the house he was looking for in Colinton. He had put his summer hat and sunglasses on.

He walked up the path to the front door of the detached house, looking around at the flowers in the front garden.

The door was answered after the second ring of the doorbell. He smiled at the old man.

'You know I don't like to be kept waiting, Thomas,' he said, the smile kept firmly in place, just in case some nosey old bastard next door was peeping past their curtains.

'Sorry. I was in the kitchen making a tea. Please come in.'

Thomas Burke was enjoying his retirement from

the psychiatric hospital, spending time with his roses and his books and watching the odd bit of TV. And he was utilising the library next door more than he used to.

'This is a nice place you have here. Did I tell you that the last time I was here? I can't remember, it was so long ago.' Subtly reminding the man of their previous connection. 'But every neighbourhood in Edinburgh is changing. They'll pull anything down now and turn it into flats. Maybe they should close all the schools so people can teach their kids at home. That way they'll have even more flats to sell. It's disgusting, Thomas. Somebody's getting their fat wallet lined somewhere.'

'Please have a seat in the living room,' Burke said, pointing the way to the room, which was unnecessary, as the patient had been here before.

'Nonsense. You go and put your feet up. I'll make the tea. I always make it when I come round. Remember the brandy we put in it the last time?' The patient laughed and Burke joined in.

'Go and put your feet up,' the patient said. 'I know where everything is.'

'Jess loved doing this sort of thing,' Burke said. 'When she was alive.'

'God rest her beautiful soul, Thomas.'

Burke headed to the living room while the patient went into the kitchen through the back of the house and got the kettle on. He found the tea bags and then took the jar of coffee out of the cupboard. After he'd poured the hot water into the two mugs, the patient added some powder to Burke's mug. Enough to kill an elephant, his old mother would say. The only poison he added to his own drink was milk.

He took them back to the living to the living room where Burke was sitting and handed the old man his fancy cup with whatever piss water was in it. Some kind of herbal tea that doubled up as concrete cleaner no doubt.

'I'm here because we have a problem. And it involves you.'

'Really? In what way?' Burke said, and the patient noticed a little clink as Burke's cup rattled in its saucer.

'Some police officers went to the hospital with a warrant yesterday and gathered up the video tapes of the Lizzie interviews.'

'Good God. That's not good. But rest assured they won't find anything incriminating on them. I took care of the camera like you told me to.'

'That's the problem, Thomas: you didn't. God knows what you actually did, but there they were in full technicolour. You didn't do a thing, and you were supposed to get rid of the tapes with the interviews you did with Lizzie. Tell them they were corrupt and just toss them. But no, there they were, large as life –'

'I thought they were corrupted,' Burke interrupted. 'I fiddled with the camera.'

The patient held up a hand. 'You did fiddle with the camera, then you were to go to the tapes and get rid of them, which you assured me you had done. Turns out you hadn't.'

'I was scared I'd get caught. I didn't destroy them.'

'Clearly.' The patient shook his head. 'Now I need to know what Lizzie said to you. Cast your mind back to when you were talking to her about the Andy Watt murder and the attack at McNeil's house.'

Burke sat back in his chair. The only sound was the ticking of a grandfather clock out in the hall. The patient hated grandfather clocks and thought they were only useful for starting a bonfire with.

'While there's still daylight left,' the patient urged.

'Yes, yes, I remember now. She said that she

didn't kill Watt but she saw who did, and that she was sent by somebody to McNeil's house.'

'Did she mention who sent her?'

'She just said "she" sent me,' Burke said. 'Anybody seeing the tape will know she means her mother, Maggie Parks.'

'Stepmother,' the patient corrected. 'And that's all?'

'That's all.'

The patient nodded and smiled. 'That's great, Thomas. Sorry to bother you. I just wanted to make sure that nothing got back to you.'

'I appreciate all you did for me back then.'

'We looked after each other.' The patient stood up. 'Can I use your bathroom before I go?'

'Of course. You know where it is.'

The patient left the room and went into the bathroom and flushed the toilet. When he came back out, Burke was sitting in his chair, his back arched like he was being electrocuted, but the patient knew the old man was overdosing on the fentanyl.

He pulled on nitrile gloves, then took his mug through to the kitchen, rinsed it and the spoon he'd used for the coffee, then dried both and put them away. He wiped down the coffee jar. Then he went back for Burke's mug and cleared everything away, making it look like the old man had never had a cup of tea. They would find the fentanyl in his system, no doubt, but the patient wasn't a man given to helping the law. He dried his gloved hands on a towel so he could take them off and take them with him.

One final look in the living room.

Thomas Burke was now with his wife. The patient hoped they were having a good time together. It had been a pleasure working with the old man. But that chapter was closed now.

FORTY-TWO

Miller was in the incident room talking about the videos when a young woman came in. At first glance, she looked like a boxer who had walked in off the street.

Stewart looked at her. 'Help you?' he said.

'Who are you?' she said.

Harry could see there was going to be a battle of the wits which the woman wasn't going to win, but she might have won a fist fight. It could go either way.

'Marj, this is Detective Superintendent Calvin Stewart, our new MIT boss.'

'Aw, right. Pleased to meet you, sir. I just wanted a wee word with yer man there.'

'This is Marj from the drugs squad,' Harry said.

'That makes sense. You play a good undercover role,' Stewart said.

'I'm no' undercover.'

Stewart gritted his teeth. 'You'll need to introduce me to your boss. Soon.'

Harry stepped forward. 'Marj, what's up?'

'The guy who got an ice pick in his eye the other night, Dale Wynn? He's known to us. He's been buying fentanyl from one of the gangs through in weegie land' – she looked at Stewart – 'I mean, Glasgow, but he's no' been making the purchase himsel'. He sent somebody through to buy it.'

'Hamish McKinley?'

'Aye, that's him. We didn't make our move, because we're building a case against them.'

'They're both deid,' Stewart said.

'The weirdo as well?' Marj nodded and made a face. 'Didn't know that.'

'Was Wynn selling it?' Stewart asked.

'I think he was just using it. We don't have any tips about him selling it, but obviously he didn't want to get caught buying it, so he got the other one to do the dirty work.'

'Thanks for the tip,' Harry said.

'Nae bother. Later.'

'Tell your boss to give me a ring,' Stewart said, 'before I have to come looking for him.'

'The drugs squad are a bit mental, sir,' Elvis said once Marj had left.

'I'll show them fucking mental. She looks like she smokes some of the shite she takes off the streets. I don't care if she rams a fucking needle into her arm, she won't be strolling in here like she owns the place from now on. I'll give her fucking drugs squad.'

Nobody argued.

'So that Wynn bastard was a druggie, eh?' Stewart said. 'We should go back and talk to his girl-friend and his ex-wife. And McKinley was coming through to our patch to buy the shite for him. Some-body wasn't pleased with them.'

'Rival gang, maybe?' Dunbar said.

'Possibly, but why would they kill them if they were just buying it for personal use?' Evans said.

Miller stepped forward. 'Why would McKinley get involved with Wynn in the first place?'

'I have no idea,' Harry said. But there was some-thing gnawing away at him. 'From the phone call earlier, we know we have three dead men who were arrested by me in the past. Wynn as a protestor, Hamish McKinley for exposing himself in a public toilet and Bobby Livingston on drugs charges. All of them arrested by me, all of them walking free. I'm the connection. Coincidence? I don't think so.'

Miller got Harry's attention. 'We watched hours of footage from the hospital, and there's nothing incriminating on it regarding Lizzie. She didn't confess. Nothing. She said she saw the van driver who killed Andy Watt. Just ramblings. But one strange thing I noticed: the old doctor who was interviewing her, Thomas Burke, he stepped up to the camera before Lizzie came into the room and touched it, almost as if he thought he was tampering with it, but nothing changed. Then when she was out of the room, he did it again.'

'Why would he touch the camera?' Harry said.

'He's an older bloke. Maybe he saw somebody do it that way on TV or something. But I'd like to go and have a word with him.'

'Okay. See if Jimmy and Robbie want to go and have a wee ride in the car with you, get them some fresh air. Oh, and Frank, I wanted to ask you: you haven't been in the flat again recently, have you?'

'No. Why?'

'Nothing. I just...nothing. Don't worry about it.' *It's just that somebody took a photo of me and Alex out of a unit drawer, broke it and drew Xs on Alex's eyes.*

Miller walked away just as Harry's phone rang.

'Hello?'

'*DCI McNeil?*'

'Speaking.'

'*It's Ewan Gallagher form the Sick Kids'. Can I have a word with you?*'

'Of course, go ahead.'

'*I don't think we should be talking about this on the phone. Walls and their ears and all that.*'

'How about lunchtime? I'm having lunch in town. I can meet you.'

'*Sounds good. My pal Bingo and I are having a half day. Is it okay if he's there?*'

Harry looked at his watch. 'Of course. I have to interview somebody at one o'clock. Can you meet me before that?'

'*Twelve? I can shoot away early.*'

That gave Harry time to get up there, find a parking space and...what? He couldn't meet in a pub. Maybe he could if he didn't drink.

'Indigo Yard. I can eat, but I can't drink alcohol. I'm meeting somebody close to there.'

'*I'll be as close to it as I can. I'm leaving now.*'

'See you there.' Harry hung up and took Jimmy Dunbar aside. 'I have to go meet a couple of people.

Keep Calvin off my back, will you, pal? We'll have a few beers tonight.'

'Nae bother.'

Harry slipped out the door, a sinking feeling in his gut. He wished he had never started the ball rolling with Ewan Gallagher, but it was too late. Or was it? He could call and cancel, but he knew he wouldn't. He wanted to hear what the younger man had to say.

FORTY-THREE

'Aye, aye, what's with all the polis cars?' Dunbar said from the passenger seat. Miller was driving and he pulled in behind the ambulance on Thorburn Road, in Colinton.

The three of them got out of Miller's car and they walked up to a uniform, who stepped forward when he saw them approaching the house.

'DI Miller, what's going on here, son?'

'Sudden death, sir.'

Dunbar and Evans showed their warrant cards.

'Who found him?' Dunbar asked.

'His housekeeper. The old boy was on the living room floor when she found him. She's in a right state.'

'Is she inside?' Evans asked.

'She is, sir, yes. The duty doctor is still in there. I must admit I'm surprised to see three senior officers attend a sudden death.'

'We were here to speak to the owner of the house,' Miller said. 'Has his identity been confirmed?'

'Yes. There are plenty of photos in there.'

Miller led them inside and they found the doctor in the living room with the corpse of Thomas Burke. Miller recognised the medic as one of the police duty doctors, and he introduced Dunbar and Evans.

'Any idea of what it was, Doc?' Miller asked.

'I thought it was probably a heart attack when I first came in here, but to be honest, I'm not so sure now. See the way his body is lying, with his back arched even though he's on his side? I'm having a guess here, but I would say that he's overdosed.'

'Overdosed?' Dunbar said.

'Aye. When somebody's having a massive heart attack, they tend to clutch their chest and go into the foetal position, not arch their back like that. Of course, I'm not a pathologist, but I've seen it before in known junkies.'

They heard the crying coming from another room.

'There's a FLO in there with the housekeeper,'

the duty doctor said. 'I told her to take the old woman away from Dr Burke here. Shame. He was a nice old guy. Enjoying retirement, but not enough of it.'

'His wife died in tragic circumstances, didn't she?' Miller said.

'Jess, aye,' the doctor said. 'She was mugged by a few of those wee bastards with their tracksuits on. They grabbed her bag, and instead of letting it go she held on, and one of them yanked it and she fell over and banged her head. She never regained consciousness and poor Thomas there had to switch off the life support. Let me tell you, Frank, if that happened to my wife, the little bastards would be getting their life support turned off. The main one, some wee bastard, eighteen years old, was charged and you know what he got? Community service. I spoke to Thomas not long after and he was livid. Community service. They need birched, if you ask me. I'm old school, just like your old man, Frank.'

'Aye, that is tragic, right enough. Poor woman. But that's the state of play right now: we catch them and the courts slap their wrist.'

'Do you think Dr Burke could have turned to drugs to ease the pain of losing his wife?' Evans said.

'Anything can happen, son,' the doctor replied. 'I

wouldn't rule it out. We were friends, see, and I've never known Thomas to take anything stronger than a good malt. But you never really know what's going on in somebody's heid.'

'With everything that's been going on, maybe we should have forensics swing by and have a look,' Miller said. 'What do you think, sir?'

'I think that might be a good idea,' Dunbar said. 'I'll let you call it in.'

Miller took his phone out and called control, putting in the request.

FORTY-FOUR

'Be on your best behaviour, for God's sake,' Ewan Gallagher said, driving his Audi TT down from the hospital.

'I'm always on my best behaviour,' Bingo assured his friend.

'Well, that's shite for a kick-off, isn't it?'

'I was on my best behaviour last night, wasn't I?'

'Barely. I mean at the end, you were bragging about how many glasses you could carry on your bell-end.'

Bingo looked at Ewan through his red glasses. 'Have a word with yourself. I never said that.'

'You'll never know.'

'Lyin' bastard.' Bingo started playing around

with the seat controls while they were stopped at a traffic light.

'Do you have to touch everything?'

'This is a nice wee motor, I have to admit. Perfect if you were a hairdresser.'

'Shut your hole. You're between cars right now, aren't you?'

'I am. Why waste money on something that's going to kill the planet one day?'

'I'll die long before the planet does, so I'm going to enjoy myself.'

'I'm putting money away for an electric car.'

'Christ, Bingo, you can afford one right now.'

Bingo spluttered. 'Afford a car? I'm not living at home like you, paying no bills, no rent, no nothing.'

'Hey, I help my old man. I'm saving for my own place again. My ex screwed me to the wall.'

'Screwed the bin man as well.'

'This is just a treat to me. Maybe Chrissie will be impressed by it,' Ewan said.

'It's a bit tight for her kids in the back.'

'What? Kids? Who says she has kids?'

'I do,' Bingo said. 'She never brought it up last night?'

'Of course, she didn't bring it up. God Almighty.

Kids. I don't want kids now, especially since I saw what Cassidy's daughter turned out like.'

'She's water under the bridge. You'll like Chrissie's kids; they're five and seven.' Bingo looked over his shoulder. 'Maybe they *could* squeeze into those wee seats after all.'

'Shite. I'm not having some wee radge tossing popcorn about in the back, kicking the seat and pissing his pants.' Then a thought struck Ewan. 'Is she married?'

'Was. Well, technically still is, but she's put in for a divorce. She wants it to come through before he gets out.'

'Gets out of where?'

'Prison,' Bingo said. 'He's in the Bar-L. Right nut job he is. Took a chainsaw to four guys.'

'Right, that's it, I never want to see her again. Fucking chainsaw. You might have told me.'

'You never asked. You're the one who wanted me to get Lexi to ask her out on a foursome.'

Ewan drove the rest of the way in silence, thinking up excuses for Chrissie should she call him, excuses ranging from he was suffering from monkeypox to he had been called up in the draft. She hadn't given off the vibe that she was a doctor and held a PhD the previous night, more that she knew how to dance on a table in a bar without falling and breaking a hip. He should have known.

They parked round the corner from Indigo Yard and walked along to the bar.

Harry sat in the bar at a table with a glass of Coke, nursing it. The lunchtime crowd were in, boots and suits and young women counting the hours until Friday night, the gateway to the weekend.

Morgan sent him a text. *See you tonight?* He sent a reply, of course. Morgan was all about the emojis, but he couldn't do it every time. To him, it felt stupid.

He thought about the gallery along the road, closed down now after some shenanigans by the previous lessee, whom Harry had helped to close down. He knew who might be interested: Chloe Walker, an artist he'd met while living down in Newton Stewart last year. She was an artist and needed a bigger gallery.

As he took a sip of his Coke a man came over and asked if anybody was sitting at his table and Harry explained he was waiting for somebody. The man gave him a *chancin' bastard* look before going back to the bar, where he and his mate stood and eyed up the table. Just then, Ewan and Bingo came in.

'What are you having?' Harry asked as the men sat down and the two guys at the bar lost interest.

Harry got their bottles of beer and put them on the table where the men were sitting.

'I have a meeting at the gallery next door in thirty minutes or so. Sorry to rush you, but –'

Bingo held up a hand. 'It's okay, Chief, we understand.'

'Bloody respect, Christ. Chief.'

'He's a chief inspector.' A torrent of abuse flowed out towards Ewan, but only in Bingo's head. Instead of saying it, he shook his head and made a Benny Hill face, which he couldn't really pull off with the red glasses. Instead, it was a *Bono with itchy piles* look.

'You wanted to speak to me about Morgan,' Harry said.

'I was thinking about her after you came to see me,' Ewan said. 'I mean, I know she's your girlfriend and I don't mean any disrespect, but you said she told you that she transferred after David died. And she found out he was cheating on her. Well, to be honest, Harry, Morgan was seeing somebody shortly before David died.'

'We're not a hundred per cent sure mind,' Bingo added, 'but he was at the hospital a lot. And they were often seen in the canteen together. Nobody came out and asked her if he was her boyfriend, but it was assumed.'

'What if it was all innocent?' Harry said. 'What if he was a doctor, or a doctor from another hospital who she had a coffee with when he came to visit?'

The other two men looked at each other before looking at Harry. 'Because he was a detective, like you.'

Harry let that sink in for a moment. 'You're sure?'

Ewan nodded. 'I mean, it's not for us to gossip, but you came to me asking about it all. It went on for a while, as far as we know. He never came along to any formal thing we had, like a Christmas party, and she never introduced him to us.'

'Did you ever find out his name?'

Ewan quickly looked at Bingo before answering. 'Stan Webster.'

Harry was still thinking about former DCI Stan Webster when he left Indigo Yard. He'd arrested the man a couple of years back after they'd discovered he'd committed murder years before. And now he'd found out his girlfriend might have been sleeping with him. Jesus.

Harry saw the blonde woman standing further along, waiting for him. Chloe Walker. It had been a while since he'd spoken to her, and as she smiled and waved at him, he smiled back, genuinely pleased to see her.

'Harry McNeil,' she said, hugging him. 'You look so good.'

They parted.

'You look terrific too, Chloe. You lost weight?'

'I have, and thanks for noticing. I joined a gym. And I met a nice young man, Malcolm. We've been seeing each other for a couple of months now.'

'Beard? Glasses? Dark hair, about five-ten?'

'How do you know that?'

'He's skulking about on the other side of the road.'

'He's not as good as you at surveillance work, obviously.'

'Does he want to come over and join us? Or is he scared of coppers?'

'I think he ought to be scared of you.'

Harry laughed. 'Tell him I won't bite him. Introduce me to him, and then you can invite me along for a drink one night and I'll give him the *If you hurt her, I'll kill you* speech then. I don't have time to do it just now.'

Chloe waved Malcolm over and the man walked over to join them.

'Hi,' he said. 'I was just waiting for Chloe to finish business.'

'Malcolm, this is DCI Harry McNeil. Harry, this is Malcolm.'

'Pleased to meet you, Malcolm,' Harry said, shaking hands. *If you touch her, it's not me you'll have to worry about. Her ex-husband's an assassin and he's in the wind.*

'And you, sir.'

'You're an artist,' Harry said, not as a question.

'I am. How can you tell?'

'Paint under your fingernails.'

'You get paid to be observant,' Malcolm said. 'Yes, I met Chloe at a gallery. She displayed some of my paintings in her own gallery and things took off. So now we're going into this gallery together as business partners.'

'Great,' Harry said. 'I hope it works out for you both. I think this is Mr Welsh now.'

The older man looked like a lawyer and was carrying a briefcase.

'You must be Mrs Walker?' he said to Chloe.

'Yes. My friend DCI Harry McNeil, and Malcom Struthers, my business partner.'

'Please come inside,' Welsh said. 'This place is already set up to be an art gallery. It was once a pub and restaurant, many moons ago.'

They went inside, and Harry remembered being here just a few months ago, when the previous tenant wasn't staying within the boundaries of the law.

Chloe and Malcolm started walking around while Welsh put his briefcase on a table.

'Mrs Walker told me how much you were asking for the lease on this place,' Harry said.

'Very reasonable,' Welsh agreed. 'The owners are keen to get a new tenant in as soon as possible. There are a lot of interested parties for this place. It's only been on the market for a couple of weeks and already a dozen people have been to look at it –'

'Let me just stop you right there,' Harry said. 'I worked the case here. There were three bodies found in the cellar. This place was the scene of some horrific murders. Is that in the brochure?'

'Well...no...it's just that –'

'I think your client is asking way too much, considering. If people find out what a bloodbath it was downstairs, then they'll go running for the hills. My friend wouldn't have set foot in here if she had known. I mean, what if he comes back? What if that wasn't his first time butchering people? This place will sit empty for years, gathering dust, and your client will be left with a property he can't lease. If he tries to sell, then they'll have to disclose what went on in here.'

'I mean –'

'Call him, your client, the man you represent,

and tell him to knock off a few hundred every month, or my friend walks.'

'You said she didn't know.'

'She will do in two minutes when I tell her.'

'That isn't strictly how we do business,' Welsh said. 'As a police officer, you should know that.'

'As an estate agent,' Harry replied, 'you should know you have to disclose this kind of shit. I'm not saying your client *has* to lower the price. We're just negotiating. But think back to how many people are really interested in this place.'

Welsh walked away and made the call. Harry could hear the mumblings from where he waited. Then the old man came back.

'He agrees to your terms.'

'What terms?' Chloe said, coming back from the tour.

'Mr Welsh said his client is eager to move this place today, so he's going to reduce the monthly rent.'

'For one year,' Welsh added quickly.

'For one year,' Harry said.

Outside, Welsh took off while the other three stood around.

'I told you he would listen to me,' Harry said.

'Bloodbath,' Chloe said. 'I love it.'

'I mean, there were dead bodies down in the basement.'

'Dead bodies?' Malcolm said. 'In the basement?'

Harry just looked at him. 'The money I saved you can pay for your electric bill every month for the next year.'

Malcolm shrugged. 'What's a few dead bodies? I'm sure there were a lot of spirits in there before.' He grinned. 'Get it? Spirits. Because it was a pub.'

Chloe groaned.

'Just as well you're an artist,' Harry said, 'because I don't think you would make it in stand-up comedy.'

FORTY-SIX

The forensics team were fussing about in Dr Burke's house, not treating it like a crime scene but having a look around and taking photos. One of the fingerprint techs was going around taking samples, 'just in case'.

'What's your gut telling you, Frank?' Dunbar asked. Evans had stepped outside to see where they were at with knocking on some doors around the doctor's house.

'I had met the man a few times when we had prisoners taken to the hospital for evaluation,' Miller said. 'He seemed like an old-fashioned bloke, you know what I mean?'

'Aye. A different generation. Like my old man – wouldn't be taking fucking crack. Just like your old man too, and not just because he's a retired copper. It's just these filth buckets who are into all that crap nowadays. So I can't see Burke taking fentanyl to get his jollies. He would know just how dangerous it is.'

'You're right. One grain too many and you're away to meet your ancestors.'

'Can you go and see what Robbie's up to?' Dunbar asked. 'I hope he's no' giving his spiel to some lassie when he's supposed to be working.'

'Aye, I'll go.'

Miller walked out into the afternoon sunshine. Evans was with a couple of uniforms across the street, talking to a woman. She was elderly and wearing a knitted twin set with pearls at her neck. She was holding on to them like one of the uniforms might nick them.

Miller crossed the road. Evans turned round when he heard Miller approaching.

'This lady says she saw a man coming out of the house a while ago.'

'What did he look like?' Miller asked.

'He was medium build, wearing a straw hat and sunglasses, and he had one of those, and I quote, "silly little beard things on the front of his face". Like he couldn't grow a full beard, she says.'

'A goatee?'

'Sounds like it,' Evans replied.

Miller stepped closer to the woman. 'Sorry to bother you with all the questions, but have you seen that man before?'

The woman shook her head back and forth, and to a casual observer standing across the road, it might have looked like she was saying 'No, you can't have my pearls' to the four men who were trying to rob her.

Then Dunbar shouted across to Miller and Evans, urging them to come back over. When they got inside Burke's house, Dunbar took them aside.

'This is weird. The tech doing the fingerprinting said that one place that everybody overlooks is the cistern handle. There was a print on it. The house-keeper said she cleans the whole house every week, including the toilet, and if there's a print there, it should only be Dr Burke's – unless he's had a guest round, of course. Now, she cleaned the toilet yester-day, so if the print isn't his, then he must have had a guest between yesterday afternoon and now.'

'The old woman across the road said she saw a man leave here earlier. But surely if he had a guest, then both their prints would have smudged each other?' Evans said.

'You would think,' Dunbar said. 'But the main

bathroom there is like the guest bathroom, as Dr Burke has an en-suite bathroom that he uses, keeping the main one for his friends when they come round on a Saturday sometimes. So if he had a guest, he would direct them to that bathroom, and that's where we got a hit. The tech has a scanner and he put the print in, and it got sent to whatever lab they use or wherever prints go to die, and the result came back in five minutes.'

They stood around, looking at Dunbar.

'Who does it belong to?' Miller asked.

'A man who's in prison right now. An ex-copper who you helped to arrest, according to his report Stan Webster.'

FORTY-SEVEN

'Well, well, second time in a week,' Maggie Parks said. 'I should feel privileged. Wait – I'm in prison, so better luck next time.' Her face was full of anger, but Harry let it wash off him.

He sat down at the table across from her. He had told the officer to leave the room, that he'd be fine. Would he, though, if Maggie came out swinging? She wouldn't do that. He'd met women before he knew instinctively who would do that, but not Maggie Parks. She was more into playing mind games.

'We were having a conflab this morning,' he said. 'We watched some videos of the interviews Lizzie did with Dr Burke. Nice man. He sat down and told us all about the little chats he had with her.'

Maggie took in a deep breath and sighed. 'No, you didn't. That's patient–doctor confidentiality.'

'Oh, I agree. But Lizzie's dead. That doesn't count now. And now the good doctor is retired, it didn't take much coaxing for him to start talking about his work. You know what it's like when an old boy retires; it takes a lot of adjustment. He's been retired for less than six months. He misses the game, the verbal sparring with a patient. The mental games to play. So when they get the chance to talk about the professional life that they just walked away from, it's like they never left when they get going. He was happy to talk to us. But I feel bad.'

'You feel bad that you conned an old bloke into talking to you. You should, Harry McNeil.'

'No, not about that. I feel bad that he collapsed after we left.'

'Dr Burke's dead?' Maggie looked shocked.

'Oh, no, he's not dead. Luckily, his housekeeper came in moments after it happened, and they got him to the hospital in time. He's going to be fine. He just had a fainting spell. His blood pressure was a bit low. No, he'll be back home later tomorrow. They're just keeping him under observation for a little while.' Harry hoped Maggie wouldn't see through the lie.

'Oh. That's something at least.'

'We'll speak to him over the weekend.'

'Hopefully, he'll tell you what Lizzie told him, about the person she said wanted to kill her.'

'Who told you said something?'

'Ben, Lizzie's boyfriend,' Maggie said. 'He's been in here a couple of times. Nice lad. I would have loved nothing more than them getting married.'

'I'm sure Dr Burke will tell us more when he gets home tomorrow. But there's something else I'd like to talk to you about.'

Maggie yawned and sat forward, putting her folded hands on the tabletop. 'Go on then, Harry. I'm all ears.'

'Stan Webster.' He looked closely at her face, watching for any sign that the name would make her twitch or move in any way that indicated she knew what he was talking about. But there was nothing.

'What about him?' she said.

'I didn't know he was dead.'

'Why not? It's common knowledge.'

'Not that common. I don't know anybody who knows he's dead.'

'It was cancer, I heard,' Maggie said. 'Stage-four lung cancer. He died six months or so later.'

'You know a lot more than I do.'

'We hear things in here. We throw parties when

we hear that another one of you bastards has popped it.'

'You were one of us, Maggie. You worked for Police Scotland.'

'I didn't put innocent men behind bars.'

'Is that what Stan was? Innocent?' Harry could feel his cheeks burning now. 'He confessed to murdering his girlfriend, who was fifteen at the time when she got pregnant, and he was a man.'

'I'm not necessarily talking about him.'

'You didn't go to his funeral. I would have got a notification about that.'

Maggie shrugged. 'Why would I want to go to *his* funeral, even if they did let me? I couldn't care less that he's dead. He meant nothing to me.'

'Do you know where he's buried?' Harry asked.

'I haven't a clue.'

Harry had just wanted to hear her answer. He had already found out that Webster was buried in Warriston Cemetery.

'Did Lizzie ever reach out to you to tell you who wanted her dead?' he asked instead.

Maggie leaned back once more. 'She was delusional. She thought everybody from the Pope to the Prime Minister wanted to kill her. I wouldn't give any credence to what she was saying.'

'You just said you hope that Dr Burke will tell me about the person who Lizzie thought wanted her dead. Now you're contradicting yourself.'

'Lizzie's mind was all over the place. When she was growing up, she was always dramatic.'

'We think that a friend of hers gave her pills which she took and that's what caused her death. It's something we're working on right now, but we won't know for sure until the toxicology report comes back.'

'Maybe she just wanted something to give her a wee buzz.'

'A buzz?' Harry said. 'The friend, McKinley, is dead anyway. We won't be able to talk to him.'

'I hate to hurry you,' Maggie said, 'but I have to go. I have a class starting in ten minutes.'

Harry nodded. 'You told me the other day that Lizzie wouldn't take her own life. Hamish McKinley didn't look like he could tie his own laces without a Dummies book, so tell me who killed Lizzie if it wasn't Hamish McKinley?'

'I don't know. See you around, Harry.'

The officer came in and took Maggie away while Harry was escorted out. He didn't know exactly why he had lied about Dr Burke still being alive. It wasn't as if *she* was the one who killed him.

He was thinking about it as he drove down to Warriston Cemetery. He drove through the gates. He'd been here before, working a case with Frank Miller as a film crew shot scenes from a new TV series. And to arrest a killer and they had discovered Stan Webster's dirty secret from twenty years earlier. Now, three years later, here he was again.

There was nobody to ask where Webster's grave would be. In the new part? That would make sense, but knowing Webster, he would be playing games right up until the end.

Harry drove down the hill to the lower level and round to where the old caretaker's cottage used to be. He got out of the car and walked past some old grave-stones and stopped at the grave marker he was looking for.

Stan Webster. Died six months ago. Harry read the names above: Webster's mum and dad.

He thought he heard a branch snap. It was noth-ing. But as he looked around, his mind went back three years, to the time they had cornered Webster. Back then they had spoken about the gravestone that Webster had pushed on top of his girlfriend, killing her. They had been standing at the spot where the poor girl had died twenty years earlier. And now Harry was standing here once more. He realised that the gravestone that had been pushed on top of the girl was Webster's own family gravestone. He had brought her to this exact spot.

Harry looked at the name again. If Stan Webster was in the ground, then why was his fingerprint on Dr Burke's toilet cistern?

'You had us all fooled, didn't you, Stan?' he said. 'But how?'

FORTY-EIGHT

Stacey Mitchell was sitting watching TV when Darren came into the living room.

'I'm making fish suppers for tea. You want the usual?'

She didn't answer. She couldn't even look at him for the tears filling her eyes. One overflowed and ran down her cheek. He saw what was going on and came over and sat beside her on the settee.

'Come on. It's going to be fine.' He put his arm around her shoulders.

'I ruined everything by going down there,' she said.

'No, you didn't.'

She turned into him and started crying hard and

he held on, being racked by her sobbing. After a few minutes, she stopped and pulled away from him.

'Sorry, I got your shirt wet.'

Lesley came into the room. 'What's all this then? Why are you crying?'

Stacey's eyes were red, wet and puffy. 'I've been stupid. I've ruined everything for everybody.'

'Oh no, you haven't. Come here.' Lesley sat down beside Stacey and put a hand on hers. 'Everything's going to be fine. These things take time.'

Darren got up and left the room.

'How do we know, though?' Stacey said. 'Are we going to stay here for the rest of our lives, or are we going to keep on moving?'

Darren came back with a box of tissues and Stacey took some out and thanked him before dabbing at her eyes.

'We'll be fine,' Darren said. 'No harm, no foul. Let's get our fish suppers, then we can go to the pub and have a few beers as usual.'

'I'd like that. Maybe I'll chase them with a bottle of vodka.'

Darren laughed. 'You and me both.'

'I'm really sorry for what I did. It won't happen again,' Stacey said.

'Don't give it another thought,' Darren said, smiling at her.

'God, I love you two,' she said, smiling and sniffing.

'Come on, let's get the table set,' Lesley said.

FORTY-NINE

The doctor was Terry Shapiro. Friday night had been his go-to night for getting blootered these past few weeks. Christ, he was starting to think he had done a stupid thing, but that was what happened when you made a deal with the Devil.

He was putting his jacket on, feeling the tiredness creep into his bones, and looked at his watch. Another week of telling people they were going to die.

He had told his secretary he was staying behind for a bit to go over old records, so she had left with a smile and a cheery 'See you on Monday'. She was a nice woman. Had her own family: husband, two kids. Time to do things at the weekend and unwind.

Unlike him. Shapiro earned good pay but didn't

have his wife and son anymore. They were both in the cold, wet ground.

There was a knock at the door and his heart missed a beat. Answer it or pretend he wasn't here? He wasn't in the mood to talk to the patient. Christ, what was he going to do? Sit in here and wait until the psycho had left?

'Police, Dr Shapiro. We need to talk.'

Oh my God. What was worse, them or the nutter?

Shapiro walked to the door and opened it. Two men were standing there looking at him.

'DCI Harry McNeil. This is Detective Superintendent Calvin Stewart. We need to talk about one of your patients.'

'Oh, really? Which one?'

But Shapiro didn't need to know which one. He already knew. He'd known this would come back to haunt him. And now it was.

'Lucky we caught you, Doc,' Stewart said, barging into the office.

'Actually, can this wait? I'm just on my way out —'

'Nope. Sit down,' Stewart said, and watched as Shapiro went back behind his desk. Harry closed the office door and sat next to Stewart.

'Sorry we have to get right to the point,' Harry said, 'but we need your help.'

'Of course,' Shapiro said. 'Anything.'

'Stan Webster,' Stewart said.

'What about him?'

Stewart took a deep breath through his nose before blowing it out through his mouth. 'Tell us about his treatment.'

'Well, I'm sorry, but that's privileged information.'

'The man's dead. He died of cancer. He was in prison for murder and he was brought here and you gave him treatment. And then he died,' Harry said.

'And now you're up to speed,' Shapiro said, smiling. 'Now, gentlemen, I really have to go.'

'What do you know about a man called Hamish McKinley?' Stewart said.

Shapiro looked up at the ceiling for a moment as if the answer was written up there. 'McKinley. McKinley.' He looked at Stewart. 'The name doesn't ring a bell.'

'He was murdered,' Stewart said. 'Knifed to death and left to die in a skip.'

Shapiro said nothing.

'Surely you remember Hamish McKinley, Doctor,' Harry said. 'After all, you shouted at him outside the police station when his friend had been arrested. Tommy McArthur. The man questioned about the abduction of Cormack. McArthur was released because of McKinley giving him an alibi. Now do you remember him?'

Shapiro nodded.

'You read about the case of Dale Wynn being murdered, I'm sure,' Harry continued. 'Stabbed in the eye with an ice pick.'

'Why are you telling me this?' Shapiro said, feeling his cheeks going red.

'We need to know if Stan Webster had any particular friends that he mentioned when he was getting treatment,' Harry said. 'It could be important. I know he didn't have any friends in prison; he was polis, after all.'

'Maybe he made friends when he was released. I really don't know.'

Harry and Stewart looked at each other.

'Released?' Harry said.

'He was dying. The request to be released on compassionate grounds was made by his lawyer and granted. Considering he killed somebody twenty years ago, I imagine he wasn't much of a threat.'

'Stan Webster died six months ago,' Stewart said. 'How long was he out before he popped it?'

'A little over six months,' Shapiro said.

The detectives were silent for a moment.

'Where was he living at the time?' Stewart asked.

'He was renting a small flat. He received his treatment there until he passed. A nurse came in to help him, and I was the one who pronounced him dead.'

'Where was this flat?' Harry asked, and he had a sinking feeling in his gut, something deep in his mind coming back to the surface.

Shapiro told him.

They stood up to leave, then Stewart turned to look at Shapiro.

'No disrespect, Doc, but I think you're yanking my chain. Now get this in your heid: people are being taken out. Start looking over your shoulder.'

And with that, they walked out.

FIFTY

Martin Sutherland was working on refurbishing one of the coffins he had got back from the crematorium. They'd had to stop for a while when the news did a big article on it, but luckily for him and his cohort, they'd got away unscathed. His friend had dropped the coffin off and had been paid his usual fee before driving off.

Now Martin was working on stripping it out. He would burn the lining in the stove he had over in one corner of his workshop, kept for such a purpose, but also for burning logs, if somebody came snooping. He would clean this coffin until he could eat his dinner off it and then charge another fortune for it.

He had just stripped the lining out and was getting ready to put it into the furnace when the door opened. He spun round, thinking it was a raid. But it was only the patient.

'What are you doing here?' Sutherland asked.

The patient smiled at Sutherland. 'Well, isn't that a nice way to greet an old friend.'

'Weren't you the one who said we would part ways and never look back? Well, I parted ways and never looked back.'

'I just needed to talk to you about something. Just to give you a heads-up.'

Sutherland put the lining in the furnace and watched as the cloth caught fire. He kept the door open to put more in.

'Still up to your old tricks, I see,' the patient said.

'The big conglomerates are squeezing us independents out. It's only a matter of time. I'm building up a nice we account that I can empty then bugger off to the sun somewhere.'

'Sounds good to me. I might do that myself.'

'I thought you might have done that already. Nothing keeping you here, is there?'

Sutherland kept moving, keeping himself busy. Maybe this psycho would take the hint and leave.

'Nah. Got a few things to do first before I do that.' The patient looked around. 'I have to say, this is a sad way to spend a Friday evening, Martin.'

'I've never been one for partying.'

The patient chuckled. 'I can imagine how you would chat up a lassie in the pub: *I deal with dead people all day. How about you?*'

'I'm not interested in that just now. Maybe not at all.'

'Each to their own.'

Sutherland turned to face the patient. 'You wanted to tell me something.'

'Dr Burke collapsed today. Somebody thought he was dead, but turns out he isn't. I'm not sure what to believe. However, the police might come round here.'

Sutherland was speechless for a moment. 'Come here? What for?'

'You're going to have to be careful what you say.'

'I won't say anything.'

'Good. I'm so glad to hear that, Martin.' The patient looked around. 'This place honks.'

'It's all wood-related.'

'Chemical smell.'

'We finish the coffins here by hand.'

'Get the kettle on, pal, and we'll have a brew.'

'Okay. You take the usual?' Sutherland asked. But he didn't hear a reply.

The patient was right behind him, and Sutherland felt the man's hands grab him, one hand on his collar, one hand on his trouser belt, and then he was being propelled forward towards the furnace. Sutherland screamed and tried to kick and put his hands out, but it was no good. His hands were still out when he touched the furnace and he screamed louder, reflexively taking his hands away. Then he could feel the heat on his face, and then the flames clawing at his skin, before he felt nothing.

The patient left Sutherland half in and half out of the furnace, on his knees, his top half burning.

Then the patient kicked over the cans of whatever chemicals were lying about, making sure one spilled over and made its way towards Sutherland's body.

The funeral director's suit was burning, and the flames crept closer to the floor.

The patient heard a whoosh as he stepped out the door into the warm summer evening.

Driving down the road, he could see the smoke getting thicker in his rear-view mirror.

FIFTY-ONE

Harry sat with his feet up on a desk as Evans and Lillian started dishing out the coffee.

'Christ, I need this,' he said, feeling his stomach rumbling.

'Right, listen up, everyone. This is what we learned today,' Dunbar said. 'But I'll let DCI McNeil tell you.'

Harry brought his feet back down, feeling tiredness hit him, even though it was early.

'We told you about DCI Stan Webster earlier. Now we know he was diagnosed with stage-four lung cancer and was released on compassionate grounds. Why we weren't told, I don't know. I think that maybe the high heid yins were told, but it didn't trickle down to us. Anyway, he died six months ago. But before he was released, his lawyer procured him a rented flat that was on the market. My flat in Comely Bank. I didn't know because a company does the letting for me and it was a lawyer dealing with it. I'm not given the names of the tenants. There was nothing to be suspicious about. God knows how the lawyer came to be letting my flat, but I think he was being manipulated by Stan Webster. So Webster ended his days in my flat.'

'Sick bastard,' Dunbar said, sipping his own coffee.

'Sticking two fingers up to you one last time,' Julie said.

Harry nodded. 'Lizzie's boyfriend brought me some drawings the other night and I, along with Jimmy and Robbie, had a look through them. Ben, her boyfriend, said that the drawings were just that, drawings. But Lizzie drew a man who looked like Colonel Sanders before he went grey. I think she saw him and recognised him.'

'Who?' Miller asked.

'Stan Webster,' Harry said. 'I don't think he's dead. I know that sounds crazy. But listen...when Morgan and I were having dinner the other night, we got into our cars, and I looked over to a passing bus and a guy looked over to me and smiled from inside the bus. He was wearing a straw hat and had a goatee. That's the description of the man seen coming out of Dr Burke's home before he was discovered dead. I think it's Webster. But I also told Maggie Parks that Dr Burke wasn't dead, just to play with her head a bit.'

'You think she's in touch with him?'

'I don't know. But I also found out that Morgan Allan knew Webster and was seen speaking to him in the hospital. Then she moved to the Royal Edinburgh. What if he visited her there too and therefore would have met Dr Burke?'

'How would Webster fake his own death?'

'With the help of the doctor and the funeral director. That's why DSup Stewart is away out to Dalkeith to talk to the funeral director with Charlie and Elvis. We can't accuse him of anything, but if he thinks that Webster is killing people, then he might admit to faking the death, or he might think about it and tell us later.'

'Or else he'll fuck off to Spain, if he's smart,' Dunbar said.

'There's that too,' Harry said.

'Where would Webster be staying, if he wasn't dead?' Julie said.

'Ben Tasker said he was staying with a friend,' Dunbar said. 'Do we know exactly where?'

'He didn't say,' Harry said. 'I haven't heard from him again.'

'He told you he was staying with a friend,' Miller said. 'He comes from Glasgow, though, so who does he know through here?'

'Nobody that we know of,' Dunbar said.

'Right, so the only person he knew through here was Lizzie. And her stepmother. Maggie Parks. And since Maggie is in prison, it's a possibility that Ben is staying in Maggie's basement flat where she lived with Paddy.'

A cold feeling shot up Harry's back until the hairs stood up on the back of his neck.

'Ben doesn't know Stan Webster from Adam. He could go to the flat and stay there. It's a two-bedroom. What if Maggie said he could stay there when he came through? And Webster's staying there too?'

'Would he like her, though?' Dunbar said. 'He must have hated her because of what she did to Lizzie.'

'He's a student, sir,' Julie said. 'Maybe he could see past it to accept her offer.'

'Let's go and have a look,' Miller said.

'We'll take uniforms too,' Harry said. 'Let's not underestimate things.'

FIFTY-TWO

'Stop fidgeting about back there,' Calvin Stewart said. 'You're making the fucking car rock about and we're doing sixty.'

Charlie Skellett was half lying about on the back seat, trying to unbutton his trousers. 'I've had something jagging my arse all day. It's getting on my wick now. I think something's stuck there.'

'The wee claw probably came off the heid of your back scratcher when you were trying to scratch your arse with it.'

'No, I still have the claw here, see?' Skellett waved the claw above the passenger seat.

'Fuck me, you nearly had my eye out with that thing. Waving it about all over the place. Smelly bastard.'

'I only use it on my leg. Sometimes on my baws if I'm sweaty.'

'Charlie, what are you doing back there?'

'I'm unbuckling my troosers so I can get the wee jaggy bit out. I think Sir Hugo was nibbling on a bone while he was lying on my troosers. I told the wife not to let him do it, but what do I know?'

'You're no' pulling your fucking troosers doon in the back of the car again, are you?'

'Just to reach in round the back.' Skellett had pulled his trousers round his knees and now he dug around for the offending sharp bit.

'Come on now, get your troosers up, for God's sake,' Stewart said. 'Elvis here's about to toss his fucking bag, looking at you in the rear-view.'

Then Elvis hit the brakes hard when a car pulled out from a side road. Stewart reached over and leaned on the horn. But they had bigger fish to fry. Skellett had rolled forward and was firmly wedged behind the front seats of the pool car.

'Aw, shite, I'm stuck. Help me, lads.'

'Help your fucking self,' Stewart said, winding the window down as they came to traffic lights and the driver in front got out of his car. It was a vicar. He came round to Stewart's side.

'I'm awfully sorry about that. My eyesight isn't

what it used to –' He stopped when he looked in and saw Skellett's skids pumping up and down as he tried to unwedge himself.

'Jesus Christ. Move your seat forward, ya fat bastard,' Skellett yelled out.

The vicar's mouth dropped open for a second. 'Oh, dear. Oh, dearie me,' he said, walking away.

'Who was that?' Skellett asked.

'Never fucking mind who that was,' Stewart said. 'Who were you calling a fat bastard?'

'You. Move the seat. My fucking heid's stuck and I'm lying on my arm.' Skellett listened for a moment. 'You pair of bastards better no' be laughing.'

Elvis couldn't answer for laughing while Stewart was chuckling to himself as the traffic started moving.

Further outside Dalkeith on the other side of the main road, they started to see smoke rising into the air. At least Stewart and Elvis did, but Skellett was still in a position where all he could see was wires sticking out from under the seat.

'Christ, look at that,' Elvis said.

'That's what the uniformed patrol will be saying about Charlie's arse if we get pulled over.'

'I hope you're enjoying this,' Skellett said.

'Meantime, I can hardly breathe. I think I'm going to pass out.'

'We're going to pass out from the fucking smell coming from the back of the car. You shouldn't be allowed out of the office except under licence.'

As they got closer to the country road that they wanted they saw the flames. Fire engines and police cars were blocking the road. A uniform walked over to their car.

'Sorry, sir, you can't come –'

Stewart held out his warrant card. 'We were coming to visit somebody in there,' he said, pointing to the workshop.

'It's fully engulfed, the fire commander said. Nobody's getting out of there, never mind in, sir.'

'Do you know if anybody was in there?'

'One of the workers lives down the road a bit and saw the smoke. He came up here and said the boss was in there working late. As of right now, there's no sign of anybody around here who might have got out, but a more thorough search will be conducted when it's safe to do so.'

'Alright, son, thanks.'

The uniform was still looking into the back of the car.

'Remember that old cartoon from a long time ago, *Wacky Races*? That's the Hooded Claw.'

FIFTY-THREE

Bellevue Crescent hadn't seen this much police activity since the shenanigans at the church next door. Uniforms piled down the stone steps where Maggie Parks had pushed Paddy Gibb and knocked on the door.

The front uniform had a battering ram in his hand, but Harry stepped forward and tried the door handle and it opened. The young constable was a big man and looked disappointed that not only could he not take the door off its hinges but he couldn't use it to skelp somebody.

'Right, lads and lassies, shock and awe,' Harry said, and six of the uniforms charged in, shouting, 'Police!'

'Ya bastard!' the big guy added.

Among the shouts of 'Clear!', one of them shouted, 'In here!'

In one of the bedrooms, not the main one but the guest room, Ben Tasker lay on his back, his arms outstretched. The blood from his throat had seeped into the covers before he had died.

'Christ,' Harry said to Miller. He looked around the room and saw clothes hanging in the open wardrobe and some personal toiletries on the dresser.

'Looks like you were right.' Harry nodded down to a holdall that was open, clothes spilling out.

In the other room, the wardrobe had clothes in it and other personal belongings.

'Now do you think Stan Webster is really dead?' Harry asked Miller.

'No.'

Harry's phone rang and he spoke to the caller before hanging up. 'That was Calvin. The funeral workshop is no more. It's going up in flames as we speak. The man we wanted to speak to, Martin Sutherland, is believed to be inside. Oh, and he said something about extracting Charlie from the back seat, whatever that means.'

'What a mess,' Miller said. 'When we arrested Webster, it was a shock to think he had killed his girlfriend twenty years before that, but he must have had the killing instinct inside of him.'

'Looks like we underestimated him.'

Then Harry's phone rang again. 'Hello?'

'Harry, it's Jessie. Sorry to bother you at work, but it's Grace. She's ill, Harry. Can you come home? I think we might need to take her to the hospital.'

'I'll be right home, Jessie. Don't panic, I'm coming.' He hung up and then he gripped Miller's arm. 'Call Jimmy and Robbie. I have to go home.'

FIFTY-FOUR

The street was quiet when Harry pulled up to his house. The sun was going down now and darkness was falling.

He parked his car but didn't lock it, not wanting the beep to sound. He walked up his front steps to the front door and saw it was ajar. Just like it had been the time when Lizzie was inside. But that time Morgan had taken care of her. He didn't think that would be the case this time.

Inside, there were no sounds of life. No TV, no movement, no nothing. He walked slowly forward to the living room, not able to believe this had happened twice.

He edged open the living room door with his foot and stepped inside.

'Here he is!' Stan Webster said. 'The man himself.'

Harry looked at the settee, where Morgan sat with her hands tied with rope in front of her. 'I'm sorry, Harry.'

'Shut up,' Webster said. He was holding a large knife near Morgan's face. He looked at Harry. 'Come on in, join the party.'

'What do you want, Stan?'

'What do I want? Fucking respect for a kick-off!' The smile was gone, and the snarl was fuelled by spit as Webster's face twisted with pure rage. 'Those dumb fucks that I killed? Dale Wynn, Hamish and that fat bastard Bobby Livingston? They were all your arrests! But you could never make anything stick. And yet you made mine stick! You arrested me and I went to fucking prison! So I wanted to show them all that you couldn't even get it right a second time around. You're the most useless bastard detective I've ever met.'

'What about Lizzie and Ben Tasker?' Harry asked.

'Lizzie had to go because she wasn't as daft as she made out. Tasker knew too much, and Lizzie told him about the flat being empty. I was staying there. It surprised me when he turned up but I told him I was a friend of Maggie's. I had to kill him before he got too nosy.'

'Lizzie said she wasn't driving the van that killed Andy Watt,' Harry said.

'She was right. It was me. I always hated that bastard.'

'Where are Jess and Grace?' Harry said, his mouth dry now.

'Upstairs. They're safe,' Morgan said.

'What do you mean, "they're safe"?' Webster yelled. 'I'll tell you if they're fucking safe or not!'

'They're not part of this,' she said.

'I'm fucking deciding this, not you.' Webster was getting wilder and more out of control by the minute. 'You know, I'm going to make this bastard watch as I kill his sister-in-law and the baby.'

Harry tensed, his body rigid, and his breathing stopped. *Just fight him. Try to save your daughter. Let him get closer.*

It was a big knife and Webster was waving it around.

'Get on your knees. Now! Or I'll kill her first!'

Harry weighed up his options: get on his knees and then fight with Webster and hope he won, or...or they were all going to die.

Harry got on his knees.

'What are you doing?' Morgan said to Webster.

'Keep your eye on him! I'm going up to kill them now. I can't leave any witnesses! I'll bring them down so he can see what I'm doing. The baby first.'

Then things happened fast. Morgan was out of her ropes and standing up with a carving knife. She rammed it into Webster's guts, once, twice, three times.

Webster went quiet, trying to speak but not managing it. Then he fell on his face on the carpet. Before Harry could get up, Morgan was standing in front of him, pointing the blood-soaked knife at his face.

'I'm sorry, but we've been planning this for a very long time,' she said. 'I won't harm the baby or Jessica, but you have to die, Harry. I've been in love with Stan for a long time. I poisoned my husband, David, on Christmas Day, that's why he crashed. If he didn't die, I would have tried again. I wanted to be with Stan, we just had to get the timing right. You took him away from me when you arrested him and he went to prison. But he had a plan, and it was working. But the stupid bastard just had to mention harming Grace. I wouldn't do that. It was always meant to be just you, Harry.'

'Christ, we slept together. Did that not mean anything to you?'

She shook her head. 'No. I just got talking to you in the pub so we could end up being with each other so that I could help Stan. I could be close to you, to keep an eye on you. He knew we slept together, you and I, but his driving force was revenge, and what was a little sex if it meant he could kill you? He should have let it go and just killed you and not mentioned the baby. But I hope you know I have to finish the job, Harry.'

Harry waited for the knife to plunge down, but then he heard shouts of, 'Drop the weapon!'

He saw her look at Webster and saw something in her face that he'd never seen when she was with him: true love.

'Together forever,' she said in a low voice and raised the knife higher.

The first shot hit her in the heart, the second in the head. She fell down onto the floor, what was left of her head resting beside Stan Webster's.

Harry was on his feet in a second as half of Police Scotland invaded his home. Upstairs, he found Grace crying. Jessica was on the bed with her, her hands and legs bound.

'I heard him. He said he was going to kill Grace,' Jessica said, crying.

'Shh. He wouldn't have got near her. Webster and Morgan are both dead. When you used our code word "Jessie", then I knew to bring the troops with me.'

Harry had told Jessica that if she was ever in trouble and couldn't speak because somebody was near her, she should use the name 'Jessie' and he would know.

He untied her and she picked up Grace and cuddled her.

When he went back downstairs, he saw a man he knew standing there smiling at him. It wasn't a Police Scotland armed-response officer who had shot Morgan after all, but a man dressed in casual clothes. There were two of them and they reeked of Special Forces.

'I made a phone call,' the man said. 'Your boys are round the corner as back-up.'

'Why are you here?'

'When I found out about that photo in your flat, with the little Xs drawn on the eyes, I made some enquiries and found out that Stan Webster died in your flat. I have Dr Shapiro in custody just now. He told us the truth after you left his office earlier this evening. But we have time to go into more detail later. I'll have a team in here tonight after we get those miscreants taken away in body bags. You'll have to be up nice and early tomorrow.'

'Why?'

'You're going on a little trip. Go and be with your daughter and sister-in-law just now. Tomorrow, up bright and early.'

FIFTY-FIVE

It was a little chillier here than in Edinburgh, with the wind coming in off the loch below. The house sat alone on the hill, and Harry could see smoke coming out of its chimney.

He got out of the Land Rover and saw the driver was going to wait. The other big SUV was behind them. It too was waiting.

He started to walk up the driveway, which was really a rough track, and then the door opened. A man and woman walked out, closed the door behind them and smiled at him as they passed; they said nothing but the big man clapped Harry on the arm in the passing.

Harry walked up to the door, opened it and walked into the welcoming warmth. He closed the door behind him. He'd been told where to go when he entered, so he walked up the length of the hallway and gently pushed on the living room door with one hand.

He stepped inside and Stacey Mitchell was waiting for him. He felt his knees start to shake and his mouth was dry. The red-haired woman who had been in the flat was now standing before him.

She was beautiful. Tears were running down her face and her lips were trembling. She gingerly walked towards him, lifting her arms.

'Hello, Harry,' she said.

Harry looked at her, tears streaming down his own face.

'Hello, Alex,' he said.

AFTERWORD

Well, that's the end of another Harry McNeil, but he'll be back in Famous Last Words, at the end of January 2023. The action takes place right where this book ends and can be pre-ordered in the following pages.

I'd like to thank my niece, Stacey Mitchell, for allowing me to use her name in this book. Also to my family who pulled out all the stops to give me time to finish this book. To Jacqueline Beard and her attention to detail. To my editor, Charlie Wilson, who once again did a brilliant job.

I just want to stress that Dale Wynn's opinion is fiction. I'm sure all the Edinburgh city counsellors are fine, upstanding citizens, but this is a crime novel, so there has to be bad guys in it, and Dale Wynn was one of them. He is not based on any person, living or dead. And none of the others are either.

Lastly, I would like to thank you, the reader for reading this book. If I could please ask you to leave a rating or review to help me out, that would be appreciated. But please, I have to ask you not to leave any spoilers regarding Alex being back. Thank you.

Until next time, stay safe my friends.

John Carson
November 2022
New York

Printed in Great Britain
by Amazon

17603561R00222